Firestar

Firestar

Anne Forbes

To Cameron,

with very best wishes,

Anne Forbes
May 25th 2010

Kelpies

Kelpies is an imprint of Floris Books

This edition published in 2009 by Floris Books
© 2009 Anne Forbes

The publisher acknowledges a Lottery grant
from the Scottish Arts Council towards the
publication of this series.

British Library CIP Data available

ISBN 978-086315-680-9

Printed in Poland

For my father

Contents

Prologue

It wasn't actually a very impressive satellite, as satellites go. Silver, shiny, vaguely round and covered with a variety of antennae that did absolutely nothing to improve its appearance, it circled the earth emitting a regular, high-pitched bleep that would have driven you crazy had you been close enough to hear it.

The bleep, however, was music to the ears of the NASA engineers at Cape Canaveral who had just launched the satellite into orbit. Crowded round the flickering banks of monitors, they breathed sighs of relief as they heard it and when the initial outburst of cheering had died down, relaxed thankfully as they tracked its path across the black reaches of space. Powerprobe, for so they had christened it, was behaving just as it should.

"Well done, Mr Easterman," the magician said seriously, his eyes taking in the smiling, triumphant face of the young man who stood by his side. Nevertheless, he frowned slightly, for given his hip appearance, he still found it hard to believe that Chuck Easterman was a scientist at all. Young, fit and tall, with hair that stood up in gelled spikes, he looked more like a pop star than anything else. Powerprobe, however, had been his idea and his reputation as the latest whiz-kid on the block was well deserved.

Chuck, for his part, looked at the professor standing at his elbow with deep respect. So much

so, that had you told him, there and then, that the
man was actually a magician, he'd quite frankly
have thought you as nutty as a fruit cake. The
word called up visions of richly robed, elderly men
who wore pointed hats and wielded magic wands
and, to be fair, there was little sign of anything
remotely magical about the dull, soberly suited
gentleman beside him. Besides which, NASA might
"do" rockets, space stations, moon landings and
the like but it most certainly didn't "do" magic
in any shape or form. Nevertheless, fantastic as
it might sound, magic was very much in the air
— and powerful magic at that.

As it happened, many months were to pass
before Chuck, totally flabbergasted, learned that
he'd had a magician on his team. And not any
old magician either, but the mighty Lord Jezail of
Ashgar: a magician of great power; a magician who
was quite determined that Powerprobe shouldn't
fail; a magician who, all along, had had his own
dangerous agenda ...

At the time, however, as Powerprobe was bleeping its way happily across the heavens, Chuck only
felt a deep sense of gratitude towards the man
who'd done so much to help him. "Thank *you,*
Professor Jezail," he answered, revelling in the
knowledge that despite the problems they'd had,
Powerprobe was actually in orbit. "If it hadn't
been for your input," he admitted candidly, "I
doubt if Powerprobe would have got off the ground
at all."

"A pleasure, dear boy," the magician smiled.
"It's been a project well worth working on and, if

Powerprobe's lasers behave as they ought, then we should be making some dramatic discoveries quite soon."

"Well done, Professor," one of the engineers interrupted, shaking his hand, "and congratulations, Chuck! You've both done a great job!"

"Thanks, Jim." Chuck grinned and, as the engineer gave the thumbs up sign, he turned to bend over a computer to check the stream of data that was coming in. "Lasers still responding, Pat?" he asked the technician who was monitoring the satellite's progress. Pat Venner looked up from the screen and grinned reassuringly. Chuck was his flatmate and he knew only too well how worried he'd been.

"Fine! Fully operational!" he replied.

Chuck's heart lifted at the certainty in Pat's voice. Despite everything, the lasers were working! "I can't believe it's all going so smoothly," he said, his voice mirroring his relief. "I've just been telling Professor Jezail, here, that at one stage, I thought Powerprobe would never make it!"

Pat looked round at the two men, his eyes glinting with amusement. "It's been some project," he allowed, "and sorting out the lasers the way you did, Professor! Well ... everybody reckons you must have waved a magic wand or something!"

Lord Jezail's eyebrows lifted as he smiled in genuine amusement. "Perhaps I did," he answered.

"It must have been something like that," Chuck nodded, not knowing just how close he was to the truth, "for, quite frankly, I could only follow your reasoning so far before I got totally bogged down."

He frowned, shaking his head. "You know, I really haven't a clue how you managed to sort that computer program out at all. At one stage I was quite convinced that the software had a virus in it."

The professor looked at him shrewdly, a slight frown in his eyes. Chuck was obviously a lot brighter than he'd reckoned and the fact that he'd even suspected a virus was a tribute to his intelligence; for there was, indeed, a virus in Powerprobe. He knew, because he'd put it there himself!

A computer scientist would probably have said that the virus lodged so carefully in Powerprobe's software was possessed of artificial intelligence. Nothing so complicated, however, had crossed the magician's mind. To him, it was a hex, pure and simple — a hex with a mind of its own that would do his bidding. Sly, nasty and malevolent, it was a mirror image of the magician himself. He called it Malfior and it knew its master.

Like all viruses, Malfior hid itself, unnoticed and unseen, in its new home and, content to follow the magician's instructions, waited patiently until it was time to go into action — which was probably why it wasn't immediately apparent that there was anything at all wrong with Powerprobe.

So, at the beginning of its mission everything went well. His task completed, Lord Jezail departed and as Chuck and the team of NASA experts settled to the complex task of satellite monitoring and data gathering, it wasn't long before the work became almost routine. Indeed, Powerprobe had been bleeping its way blamelessly round the world for about six weeks with quite satisfactory results when its lasers picked up on a mind-boggling source of power.

This was what Malfior had been waiting for. It could only be Firestar. *This* was *it*! It obeyed its instructions to the letter and, even as the laser locked on, Malfior slid down its beam to lodge itself, unnoticed and unseen, in its new home.

Powerprobe's reaction was immediate. As the laser hit the strange power source, its computers went berserk as things went monumentally pear-shaped. Everyone knew it the moment an ear-splitting shriek shattered the silence of the busy control room.

It wasn't the noise, however, that caused Pat Venner to push his chair back violently from the bank of monitors. With a cry of terror, he scrambled to his feet and, backing away, pointed a quivering finger at his screen, his voice incoherent and his face, chalk-white with shock.

"What's *that*?" he croaked wildly. "What the devil's *that*?"

1. Panic attack

Arthur, the great dragon, sat up suddenly on his enormous heap of treasure. Living in the depths of Arthur's Seat, the huge hill that dominates the Edinburgh skyline, he had always felt completely safe. The MacArthurs, the magic people who lived in the hill, looked after him well and, indeed, he was very fond of them; especially Archie who was, at that moment, perched beside him in the crook of his arm.

"What is it, Arthur?" Archie looked up as Arthur shifted uncertainly, his claws scrunching gold and jewels underfoot as he sensed danger. The dragon turned his great head to look at him worriedly. He sniffed the air and blew a cloud of smoke down his long nose. "Archie," he said, "something's wrong. I feel strange ..."

Archie got to his feet and, slipping down the side of the pile of treasure, looked round the cavern suspiciously. He knew that something must be happening, for dragons are sensitive creatures and rarely make mistakes. It was then that the force struck. It came out of nowhere and hit him hard. Archie gasped in pain, doubled up and fell to the ground, unconscious.

Arthur gave a roar of alarm as he, too, felt the powerful shock of a mighty attack. Dragons, however, have their own magic and Arthur fought back strongly. Such was its ferocity, however, that his body writhed in a dreadful spasm that sent his treasure flying everywhere. Its power shook him to the core and, with awful certainty, he realized that, strong though he was, the attack might overcome him. He was appalled. Nothing like this had ever happened to him before. His head dropped and his wings fluttered weakly as he found himself sprawled helplessly amid the heaped piles of glittering gold.

As his wonderful eyes lost their focus and his strength ebbed within him, he desperately concentrated the last of his magic on the firestones, the most special of all the jewels in his treasure. Firestones have an enchantment of their own and they responded to his call in a rippling wave that swept them up through the great pile of treasure, covering him in seconds in a layered armour of gleaming, amber brilliance.

As the comforting warmth of the firestones' magic started to seep through him, Arthur felt his strength return. Dizzy with relief, he opened his eyes, flexed his wings and prepared to do battle. Just as he was bracing himself, however, the force withdrew. He looked round the cavern in amazement. There was nothing! It had gone, just as suddenly as it had come.

"Archie," the dragon looked at the slight figure that lay doubled up on the floor, "Archie! Are you all right?"

Archie sat up slowly and looked round in dazed bewilderment. "*What,*" he said, fearfully, "was *that*?"

"I don't know," Arthur replied, sliding down towards him, shedding firestones everywhere, "but whatever it was, its magic was the most powerful I've ever felt. I thought I was going to die!"

"Me, too," Archie said, white-faced and shaken. He pulled his sheepskin jacket straight and rose unsteadily to his feet. "I still feel a bit wobbly round the knees."

"Here, put this round you," Arthur advised, hooking a necklace of firestones from his treasure with his claws. "It'll make you feel better."

Archie looped the necklace over his head and immediately regained some of his colour. "I hope the others are all right," he said, looking at Arthur anxiously. "I mean, it might not just be us that it attacked ..."

The dragon nodded. "Get on my back, quickly. We'd better go to the Great Hall and see what's happened! I hope the MacArthur is all right."

Arthur positively galloped along the tunnels that led to the Great Hall, worried that the MacArthurs might have been struck down too. When they reached the hall, the dragon came to an abrupt halt and stared at a scene of total confusion. Little groups of MacArthurs clustered here and there, still looking round nervously in case the unseen enemy struck again. Even the magic carpets seemed affected by the strange force for they were flying around haphazardly in the dim heights of the cavern, totally disorientated.

"Thank goodness you're both all right!" the MacArthur, himself, spotted them and strode across. "I was about to send Jaikie along to see how you were!"

"What happened, MacArthur?" Archie asked,

as he slipped off Arthur's back. His eyes shone
with relief as he saw Hamish and Jaikie, still looking pale and nervous from their ordeal, coming
towards him.

"Wasn't that awful?" Jaikie muttered, hugging
him briefly. "I hope to goodness it doesn't happen
again!"

"We were really worried about you," Hamish
said, his face grave and shocked. "But what was
it?"

"You'd better come and pay your respects to
Prince Casimir," the MacArthur interrupted, ush-
ering Archie forward. "He arrived just before all
this happened."

They followed him to a dais where several
throne-like chairs were grouped in a half circle.
Prince Casimir, resplendent in a cloak of dark blue
velvet, was looking into a glowing, crystal ball that
rested on a carved ebony stand. He straightened
as they approached and although he managed to
smile a welcome, his thoughts at that moment
were elsewhere. Uppermost in his mind was the
fate of his son, Prince Kalman. Had he survived?

Archie gave a sigh of relief as he saw Prince
Casimir. He was one of the Lords of the North and
a magician of considerable power. Arthur, blowing a cloud of smoke down his long nostrils, knelt
before the grey-haired, elderly figure and bent his
great head. "Welcome, Prince Casimir," he said,
"at this dangerous time."

Archie bowed low. "Prince Casimir," he said.
Then, throwing formality to the winds, a rush of
words tumbled out of him. "Thank goodness you're

here. Can you tell us what happened?" He took a
deep breath. "Milord," his voice was anguished. "It
nearly killed Arthur ... and he's a dragon!"

Prince Casimir smiled gravely at the great
dragon. "You would probably have survived,
Arthur," he said. "Dragons are pretty well invinci-
ble! But I'm glad to see you both unhurt."

The MacArthur looked enquiringly from Casimir
to the crystal. "Er ... has Prince Kalman contacted
you to say he's all right?" he asked tentatively, for
he knew that father and son were not on speaking
terms.

Casimir shook his head. "I've tried to find him,"
he admitted, "but he's hiding himself from the
sight of the crystal."

The MacArthur put a comforting hand on his
arm. "I wouldn't worry too much," he said. "We've
all survived so there's every reason to suppose that
Prince Kalman, too, is alive and well."

Prince Casimir smiled wearily. "That gives me
hope," he admitted, sighing deeply as he passed his
hand over a crystal that suddenly glowed to life.

Prince Kalman had, indeed, survived. High
above the mountains in the ice palaces of the snow
witches, he eased himself upright and thankfully
drew breath, wondering what on earth had hit
him. Never before had he experienced such a devastating attack. He glanced at the chaos around
him. It had been such a carefree scene only a few
minutes earlier for the witches had been preening
themselves before him, teasing him and asking his
advice.

Cassandra had started it. "*I* think," she'd said archly, "that we ought to change the colour of our robes. I'm fed up with this ivory and white stuff!" She paraded around with the angular strut of a model, the flounced petticoats of her dress swirling gracefully.

"What about pink?" Matilda asked hopefully, one eye rather nervously on the queen who didn't seem the least bit enthusiastic at their proposed changes.

"Come off it, Matilda," another said sourly, "we're snow witches, remember, not flower fairies!"

"It's the earth witches that are the luckiest," sniffed Henrietta. "They get to wear black ... and black is *so* elegant ..."

"Just think yourself lucky you're not a wind witch, Matilda," Horatia pointed out mischievously, "for they have the worst deal of all. Grey! Yuck!"

"What colour would *you* like us to wear, Prince Kalman?" Cassandra asked, looking slyly at the queen out of the corner of her eyes.

The prince looked amused. "I think you look very well as you are," he said idly. "If I wanted you to change anything, I think it would be your eyes. The brown stones that you wear protrude far too much. I think flat pieces of jet would look much better. It would match your hair, too," he added dryly. "If, that is," he glanced at the queen, "her majesty agrees with me."

It was as he smiled at the queen that the attack occurred. "Aaaaaaah," he gasped suddenly, sink-

ing to his knees in pain. All around him he heard
screams and cries from the witches as they, too,
doubled up in agony and sank to the floor.

Now, he looked round at the moaning figures
of the witches as they struggled to their feet.
Samantha, Queen of the Snow Witches, pulled herself onto her throne and lay back exhausted.

"What ... what happened, Prince Kalman?" she
whispered hoarsely, her long black hair a soaking
mess of half-frozen slush. "Who did this to us? I
thought I was going to lose my life ..." She looked
at him appealingly for he was, after all, one of the
Lords of the North. His appearance, however, did
nothing to inspire her with confidence; instead, it
struck cold fear in her heart. Never, she thought,
had she seen the prince so shaken and she watched
in dismay as he straightened himself with an
effort.

"I wish I knew, Samantha," he said grimly, shaking particles of wet ice from his fair hair, "but whoever did this has tremendous power." He looked
stern and thoughtful as he made his way shakily to one of the high-backed chairs, carved from
the glittering ice of the snow palace. A variety of
possibilities crossed his mind only to be rejected
immediately. His eyes looked worried as he shook
his head. "I don't know who would do this to us,"
he admitted.

His father, he knew, would probably know what
was going on and for a few seconds he thought
of lifting the hex that hid him from the world of
magic. It was a momentary weakness, however,
for his anger at the loss of the Sultan's crown still

burned within him. No, he thought grimly, there was no way he was going to ask his father!

All around the vast hall, witches were rising from a floor that gleamed wet with the sheen of water. Their delicate dresses of ivory chiffon had ceased to float round them in a froth of dancing ruffles and now hung in ghastly, sodden lumps round their ankles. Shrieks of dismay rose from the witches as they looked round and saw to their horror that the sparkle of the gleaming ice had dulled. Their palace was melting!

Samantha rose to her feet and throwing out her arms, spoke in the language of the witches. The hex she used was the most powerful of all the hexes she knew and there was a sigh of relief as a blast of icy air swept through the hall and restored the delicate tracery of carvings, pillars, arches and vaulted roofs to solid ice.

"Prince Kalman," she said, looking at him with fear in her eyes, "you must find out who or what caused this dreadful attack. If there is another, we might not survive!"

2. Hobgoblins

If you were at all familiar with hobgoblins, you would have known at once that Rumbletop was totally distraught, for the bumpy nodules that covered his goat-like little head were sprouting frantically all over the place in a seething tangle of tendrils that made him look like a demented octopus.

"What on *earth* was that?" he groaned, automatically shoving the writhing tendrils out of his eyes as he struggled to his feet. He looked round the cavern fearfully. The attack had happened suddenly, without warning and had been ferocious. "What happened?" he moaned, staggering over to Rumblegudgeon who was sitting on the ground, shaking violently. "I thought I was going to die!"

"So did I!" Rumblegudgeon whispered, his slanting yellow eyes wide with alarm. He, too, was having a bad hair day. He picked himself up off the floor and barely noticing the long, rubbery tendrils that slithered over his rather natty scarlet waistcoat, staggered unsteadily towards the monitor on the control panel where jagged streaks of red light sizzled and flashed.

His only thought was to protect Firestar, the great ball of energy that pulsed in the cavern below, for it was as one with the machine, which, he saw with rising panic, was still vibrating wildly. He'd no idea how or why humans should have targeted it but the effect had been little short of disastrous; indeed, had it lasted longer, he was sure he would have died.

"Do something, for goodness sake, before the whole thing implodes!" Rumbletop muttered, eyeing the machine apprehensively as the hall filled with anxious hobgoblins. "The pressure's dropping fast and if it falls too far, Firestar might collapse!"

"The attack came from the world outside, Rumbletop!" Rumblegudgeon flung at him as he reached the control panel. Flinging his tendrils hastily over his shoulders, he slid into the chair and concentrated on the monitor. "I saw a man on the screen just as it happened ... a human! The attack was from the outside!"

Rumbletop looked flabbergasted. "You saw a man!"

Rumblegudgeon nodded. "Haven't I just told you?" he said. "He attacked us and took the heart out of Firestar."

Rumbletop could hardly believe what he was hearing and watched anxiously as Rumblegudgeon bent intently over the control panel. Altering a few settings, he pressed the odd button here and there and, with a last look at the pressure gauge, crossed his fingers firmly.

The two hobgoblins eyed one another fearfully. The trouble was, Rumbletop thought grimly, that nothing like this had ever happened before and although he'd become close enough to Firestar to feel its moods and sometimes, even, its thoughts, no one really knew enough about the bright ball of pulsing energy to cope with anything like *this*.

Indeed, Firestar was, quite truthfully, a mystery to them all. It was rumoured, in hobgoblin circles at least, that even the Lords of the North were not quite sure how Firestar had come to be in the mountain, nor how the machine that controlled it had been built. Some spoke of a people even older than the magicians who had lived in the mountain before time began but as no one had ever found any trace of them, he didn't really know the truth of it; although, given the set-up, it was more than probable.

The only thing he knew for sure was that if Firestar were to collapse and die, the whole world of magic would collapse and die with it. Firestar was its life source and it was as he shivered, realizing just how close they had all been to certain death, that a feeling of relief swept through him — surely his tendrils were shrinking? He looked down and, as they curled up off the floor, realized that he did actually feel much better than he had a few minutes before. Was the danger passing? Was Firestar recovering? He looked at Rumblegudgeon, suddenly hopeful as he saw that the pressure gauge was rising fast. He gulped thankfully. "I think the worst's over," he whispered.

Rumblegudgeon closed his eyes momentarily, totally overcome as he realized that Firestar had, after all, managed to pull through. "I think you're right," he nodded as they both felt Firestar's strength pulse strongly through them. "Thank goodness for that!"

They turned to the machine which, although still churning somewhat nervously after its unex-

pected encounter, seemed to be slowly settling
to its normal rhythm. Nevertheless, it was only
after a good deal of clicking and clattering that the
dreadful noise finally died away and the machine
ceased vibrating as Firestar settled to a more normal rhythm.

Lights, however, still flickered on and off in
unexpected places and although the monitor now
displayed nothing more exciting than a fairly even
pulse of light that every so often jerked in a mild
hiccup, one of the series of circles that ran along
the top of the screen had lost its shape and closely
resembled a somewhat demented spider.

The two little hobgoblins looked at one another
and, as their panic subsided, so did their tendrils.
With any luck, thought Rumbletop, things might
now return to normal. Even as the thought crossed
his mind, however, he knew it for a forlorn hope.
Until they found the cause of the sudden attack,
nothing in Morven would ever be the same again.

Rumblegudgeon, too, looked at the monitor
assessingly. "Apart from that spider thing," he
pronounced, "Firestar seems to be okay. I'll check
it out more thoroughly later." He looked round
at the crowd of hobgoblins that had gathered
anxiously round the machine. "Calm down," he
said, noting their worried faces, "whatever the
force was, it only accessed us for a few minutes.
It certainly took me by surprise," he said shakily,
hitching up his short, flappy trousers. "It was the
last thing I was expecting. After all, it's never happened before, has it?"

As the hobgoblins solemnly shook their heads,

Rumbletop groaned at the thought of having to go upstairs to tell the Lords of the North that Firestar had been discovered by the outside world. He felt his tendrils start to grow again and even as he headed for the broad staircase that rose to the upper chamber of the mountain, the rubbery strands flowed behind him like a tangle of writhing snakes.

Emerging from the depths of the mountain into the majestic halls of Morven was a breathtaking experience. Lofty, spacious and majestic, the cavern glowed with a soft, blue light. Ahead of him reared the glittering silver thrones where the Lords of the North passed their days. Mostly, it must be admitted, in gentle slumber as they were so old that they tended to doze off now and then. On occasion, however, they had been known to chat idly and pore lazily over books of ancient spells. The highlight of their days, however, was when they had visitors; for not all of the Lords of the North were old men.

Rumbletop sighed enviously as he thought of the young lords, for they were proud and handsome with great estates of their own in the outside world. He shook his head sadly. The trouble was that the old lords were so boring that the younger lords didn't often visit except in an emergency. There was always great excitement among the hobgoblins when this happened for then they had a splendid show of fireworks above the mountain to mark the importance of the occasion.

As Rumbletop made his way over the vast mar-

ble floors of the Great Hall towards the thrones of
the Lords of the North, their faces grew grim as
their worst fears were realized. They only had to
look at Rumbletop to know that something, somewhere, had gone fundamentally wrong for never
had they seen his tendrils, snaking in a twisting,
tumbling train behind him, reach such a length.

Rumbletop's goat-like face surveyed them anxiously. They, too, he reckoned, must have felt the
attack for it was quite unheard of for *all* of them to
be awake at the same time. He halted as he neared
the low silver table that fronted the half circle of
high-backed, elegant thrones and bowed low to
each one in turn, waiting for them to speak.

Lord Alarid, white-haired, white-bearded and
gorgeously robed in shades of dull red, looked at the
hobgoblin through watery blue eyes and stretched
out a thin hand in greeting. "Rumbletop," he said
in a quavering voice, "we were about to send for
you. For an instant we felt a terrible weakness ..."

Lord Dorian almost sniffed. *A terrible weakness,
indeed,* he thought caustically. It certainly wasn't
the way he would have put it! He looked round at
the other Lords and knew they were of the same
mind. Like him, they had always considered themselves immortal but this attack had given them
pause for thought. What *was* this powerful force
that had rendered them helpless and their magic
useless?

"It's Firestar, milord," the hobgoblin said worriedly, "I'm afraid that someone from the outside
has discovered it."

The Lords of the North shifted in their chairs

and looked at one another in appalled silence. Lord Alban sitting straight as a ramrod was moved to speak. "Someone from the outside," he repeated, "but ... that's impossible!" Nevertheless, he was seized by a sudden feeling of dread. Firestar was their life source. No one, but no one, could be allowed to interfere with it, let alone humans.

"We must call everyone to a meeting," Lord Alarid said somberly. "The attack was extremely powerful. Everyone must have been affected and I hope no one ... well, I just hope that everyone survived, that's all. Lord Rothlan and Lady Ellan at Jarishan, for instance."

"And the MacArthurs," added Lord Alban.

Lord Alarid thought of Arthur, the huge red dragon that lived with the MacArthurs in Edinburgh. "Arthur will be all right. Dragons are powerful creatures and their magic is strong. Surely ..."

Lord Dorian could contain himself no longer. "*We* are powerful and *our* magic is strong," he interrupted bleakly, "and, until today, *we* thought *we* were immortal."

There was a lengthy silence.

"I take your point, Dorian. You are right. Any damage to Firestar affects us all. We must find out where this attack came from."

Lord Dorian nodded. "Indeed we must! And as soon as possible! You do realize, don't you, that if it happens again, we might not survive?"

As the murmur of horrified assent rustled round the curve of silver chairs, Lord Alarid rose and, gathering his velvet robes around him, moved towards the low table that lay in front of the thrones. In its centre, on an ornate stand of carved, black ebony, stood a crystal ball whose opaque interior was clouded by a swirling, white mist. Even as he approached it, however, the mist dispersed and, as the crystal glowed with a bright light, a familiar face appeared.

"Prince Casimir," Lord Alarid said grimly, "I was just about to call you."

3. Powerprobe

"As you all know, Powerprobe's orbit is set to follow a slightly different path each time it circles the earth," Chuck explained to a hastily convened committee, that afternoon. "I was in the control room at the time and the first indication that anything out of the ordinary was happening was when the tone of the bleep changed."

"Was that abnormal?" queried the chairman.

"Well, no," Chuck answered. "The tone is designed to change when an energy field is discovered; the louder the noise, the more important the find, so to speak. As you know, we've already discovered several new oil fields and some massive mineral deposits in Africa, but none of them as big as this."

"Go on," the chairman nodded.

"Well, the tone changed to an absolute shriek of sound so we knew Powerprobe had latched on to something fantastic. We were all absolutely stunned as you can imagine and rushed to the monitor. Patrick Venner was in charge and had homed in on it immediately. Whatever that energy field is, Sir, it's absolutely huge, there's no doubt about it. The readings were off the scale."

Everyone sat up, looking decidedly interested. "May we know where this source was discovered?" one of the directors asked. Thin-faced and with a nose like the beak of an eagle, he bent a penetrating eye on Chuck.

"It was in a mountain in the north of Scotland."

What could have been a sigh of relief rippled round the long table. Scotland ... at least it was a friendly country ...

"Well," the director frowned and leant back in his chair, "what's the problem? I imagine there is one or you wouldn't have called us all together at such short notice."

Chuck shifted uncomfortably but his gaze, under the spiked ramparts of his hair, was direct. "The thing is, Sir," he said taking a deep breath, "that it wasn't only the noise that freaked us out. Pat Venner saw it on his screen before we had time to take in what was going on. He let out a yell that stopped us in our tracks and ... well, before we could get to the monitor to see what was happening," he explained carefully, "he'd shoved his chair away from the screen. He was as white as a sheet and to tell you the truth, I'm not surprised. I was closest to Pat and I caught a glimpse of it before the satellite moved on ..."

"A glimpse of what?" the chairman asked.

"It was," Chuck pursed his lips, "we think ... actually, we think it could be ... an alien."

"A ... *what*?" The committee jerked to attention and eyed one another in disbelief.

"It's the only word I can think of to use, Sir. The creature we saw certainly wasn't human."

"An alien! Are you *sure*?" Everybody at the table was now sitting bolt upright, their faces intent.

"It looked something like a goat, Sir, with slanting, yellow eyes but quite frankly the resemblance ended there. Its face was hairy and it had lots of little horn-like bumps on its head. I don't know if it could see us but ... it sort of snarled at us before it disappeared." Chuck shivered at the thought, for before the picture had cut out, the creature had pulled back its lips in a malevolent grimace.

The chairman didn't quite know what to say. "You're ... quite sure about this?" he asked in a whisper. "I mean ..."

"We've got a print-out, Sir," Chuck said briefly, handing sheets of paper round the table.

"Good heavens!" the chairman echoed everyone's feelings as his eyes took in the face of the fierce goat-like creature that glared at him from the page. "I think you might be right. There's no way this ... thing ... is from earth. Just look at it!" Words failed him.

Another committee member, sitting at his elbow, leant back in his chair and eyed Chuck warily. "You're not having us on, Chuck, are you?" he queried. "It's like something out of *Star Trek*!"

"It certainly isn't friendly," another added, appalled at the baleful expression in the creature's eyes.

"Not only that," Chuck continued, "there's also the fact that it's sitting on a huge power source that we haven't yet been able to identify."

"You mean it's not oil?"

"As I said, Sir, it's nothing we can identify. The readings are a total scramble. We can't make anything of them. That's why we thought the creature might be an alien. You see, we reckon it could have come from outer space using its own power source."

There was a horrified silence.

"This," the chairman said, his voice shaking slightly, "must be kept top secret. The President will have to be informed."

A senior member of the committee, seeing problems looming, broke in at this stage. "May I suggest that Mr Easterman has Powerprobe's orbit adjusted so that it continues to pass over the source of this power?"

"Sorry, Sir, but technically that's just not a feasible option," Chuck responded. "You see Powerprobe's orbit cycle is pre-set. It'll be at least six weeks before it passes over Scotland again."

"Actually, that's probably better all round," the chairman said thoughtfully. "It'll be for the President to decide, of course, but if these creatures *are* aliens then we certainly don't want to alert them and perhaps provoke retaliation."

"And the Brits?" queried someone else, "shouldn't we ... inform them?" He tailed off as they eyed one another indecisively.

The chairman glanced round the table. "Maybe we should find out a bit more about the situation first. I ... er ... I don't know if the Brits would believe us and, well, at the moment, we don't know anything for sure, do we? What if it's all pie in the sky? I mean," he waved a casual hand, "with all due respect to Chuck, here, it might just be that Powerprobe went berserk for a few minutes and picked up on some kids' TV programme."

Expressions brightened at the thought and several heads nodded in agreement.

"If we're wrong, it could be more than a bit

embarrassing. After all, we don't want to end up with egg on our faces, do we?"

"True," Chuck nodded, albeit somewhat doubtfully.

"Then, if we're all agreed," the chairman looked round the table, "I'll suggest to the President that we investigate the matter on the ground first before taking any action." He eyed Chuck speculatively. "How would you feel about heading a team to suss out the place, Chuck?"

Chuck, feeling like he had little choice in the matter, nodded in agreement.

The committee looked at one another and glanced again at the goat-like face that stared ferociously from the print-out.

"You'll need a base, of course, but if, as you say, this power source is in the Scottish mountains then I reckon there'll be some fairly isolated properties for rent in the area. In any case, we'll set you up with everything you need as close to this mountain as we can get." He looked at Chuck gravely. "I presume you pin-pointed its exact location?"

"I did, sir," Chuck nodded. "As I said, it's in Scotland. It's a mountain in the Grampian range, not far from a city called Aberdeen."

"And the name of this mountain?"

Chuck hesitated. It was stupid, he knew, but he'd felt a strange sense of foreboding the minute he'd accessed it on the computer. "The mountain," he said slowly, "is called Morven."

4. Storms in the north

"Scotland," the TV weatherman casually indicated an area dotted with black clouds and bolts of lightning, "is unfortunately going to see the worst of the weather tonight. The violent storms we forecast this morning are already raging across the Highlands and will last well into tomorrow. Edinburgh and the Borders, however," and here his hand drifted elegantly southwards, "will be calm with just a few scattered showers here and there."

"Well," Janet MacLean said, rising to her feet, "Neil and Clara aren't having very good weather for the start of their holiday, are they? It was kind of the Grants to invite them for Easter."

John MacLean nodded. "It certainly gives us a free hand to go down to the Borders and stay with Muriel for a couple of weeks ... at least until David gets better. I'm really quite worried about him." David was his elder brother and news of his illness had taken them completely by surprise as he'd always led a healthy, active lifestyle.

"Muriel will be glad of the company," nodded his wife, picking up the remote control and aiming it at the TV screen. "It's hard work looking after an invalid."

"And I'll try and do a bit of work in that huge garden of theirs ... depending on the weather, that is," her husband added, taking one last look at the forecast before the TV screen went blank.

"Scattered showers can mean anything."

Janet put their cups and saucers on a tray and headed for the kitchen. "We'll play it by ear," she said, "and, anyway, a bit of rain won't bother Neil and Clara. They'll be too busy talking to Lewis to notice it. After all, they haven't seen him since Christmas."

Their mother was quite right. Neil and Clara hadn't stopped talking since they'd met up with Lewis and his mother at Aberdeen's busy railway station.

"Hi, Neil," Lewis greeted them. "Hi, Clara! Gosh, it's great to see you! I've been counting the days!"

"So have we," Neil said.

"Thank you for inviting us, Mrs Grant," Clara smiled. "We're really pleased to be here."

"It's lovely to have you, Clara. Lewis has been planning lots of things for you to do while you're here."

"Dad's going to the Shetlands on business," Lewis said excitedly, naming some islands that lay to the north of the Scottish mainland, "and he thought he'd take us with him. There's a ferry that does a sort of mini-cruise so that you live on the boat at night and tour the islands during the day."

"That sounds great." Neil looked at Clara in excitement. Neither of them had ever been on a cruise before.

They piled their bags onto the trolley and Margaret Grant smiled indulgently as she steered it towards the exit, listening to their excited chatter. She was pleased that Lewis got on so well with Neil and

Clara. He was an only child and, with a father in the
oil business, had never been anywhere long enough
to make real friends. Now that they were back in
Scotland things had changed, though. He seemed to
have settled well into his new school and his friendship with the MacLean children, whom he'd met in
Edinburgh, was as strong as ever. There seemed,
she thought, to be a special bond between the three
of them. They were forever calling or texting one
another and, she thought as she manoeuvred her
trolley to the exit, at least one advantage of having
them all under the same roof would, hopefully, be a
much smaller telephone bill.

What Bob and Margaret Grant didn't know, however, was the fantastic set of circumstances that
had brought the children together in the first place.
Neil and Clara's father, the park ranger on Arthur's
Seat, had always known that magic people called
the MacArthurs, lived in its depths. Neil and Clara
had played with them as children and after helping
them sort out their dragon who, at the time, had
taken to fire-raising in earnest, they had had many
adventures; for the MacArthurs had given them
magic firestones so that they could merge with
humans, birds and animals and fly on magic carpets. They were also on friendly terms with many
of the Lords of the North; great magicians whose
magic was strong and powerful. Indeed, it was
through Prince Casimir that they had met Lewis —
for Lewis had inadvertently become involved in the
world of magic and, like them, wore a firestone.

It was when they were stuck in a traffic jam
halfway down a busy street that Margaret Grant,

glancing idly at the shoppers crowding the pavement, saw a face that she recognized. Interesting, she thought, for there was no mistaking the tall young man with the strange, spiky hair who was helping to load up a 4x4 with groceries. It was after dinner, however, when the children had gone upstairs to unpack and sort themselves out, that she remembered the incident and mentioned the matter to her husband.

"Bob," she said as she stacked the dishwasher, "remember the Americans that were involved in setting up the Earth Satellite Station at Umm al Aish when we were in Kuwait?"

"Yes?" her husband looked at her speculatively. "What about them?"

"Well, I'm sure I saw one of them when I was picking up Neil and Clara; Chuck ... the one with the funny, spiky haircut."

"Chuck?" her husband's eyebrows rose. "Chuck Easterman? I wonder what brings *him* here."

"There were quite a few of them. Americans, I mean. Loading up a 4x4 with stuff from the supermarket. It looked as though they were catering for an army."

Bob Grant frowned. "I got on quite well with Easterman," he said, "but I hear that he's moved on to bigger and better things. The grapevine has it that he's involved with the space agency these days."

"Well," Margaret said soothingly. "I'm sure we'll be hearing from him soon. After all, he's bound to know you're in Aberdeen."

"Maybe," her husband said idly, rising to his feet

as a strong gust of wind rattled the window panes, "maybe not." He looked out of the window into the gathering gloom. "I think I'll put the car in the garage. The wind's getting up and the forecast isn't too good."

"Try and get the cat to come in at the same time," his wife urged. "I don't like leaving her out for too long — especially when the weather's bad."

The storm lashed Scotland all that night. Gale force winds howled through its mountains and glens with tearing ferocity while driving rain turned the thin burns that ran off the hills into raging torrents that pulled boulders from their path and sent them bouncing and tumbling into the valleys below.

As thunder rolled and lightning flashed in vicious streaks across the sky, you could be forgiven for thinking that no one in his right mind would ever have ventured out on such a night. Highlanders, however, have always been a law unto themselves and the crofter, striding the hills, knew the countryside like the back of his hand. Making his way confidently towards his house on the other side of the glen, he was well content with his night's work, for the pair of rabbits in his capacious pockets would make an excellent stew for his supper.

Nevertheless, he paused as he topped a ridge and, visited by a sudden sense of unease, stood perfectly still, his eyes searching the gloom. Although he could see nothing untoward, a sixth sense told him that something strange was happening.

The towering peaks of the mountains, lit by the occasional flash, now loomed strangely menacing before him, no longer the familiar, everyday slopes that he knew. Indeed, he hardly recognized them, so unfriendly and threatening had they become. Moving towards a rocky bluff, he pressed himself against it and waited and watched apprehensively, suddenly afraid to venture further.

An enormous rumble of thunder marked the birth of the stone giant as it tore itself in a welter of rocks, stones and crumbling clods of earth from the side of the mountain and took its first tentative steps.

The crofter's grey eyes sharpened, for his night vision was good. Something was moving on the far side of the glen. Then he saw it through a bank of swirling rain; a lumbering stone figure that stood the height of a house. Frozen with fear, he watched it walk, slowly and deliberately, with massive steps, towards the road that ran the length of the glen. Streaks of lightning illuminated the terrible figure for a brief moment before darkness fell and a sudden, dreadful, crashing roar of sound was masked by peals of thunder.

Ten minutes later, he was wondering if he'd imagined the whole thing. The storm had gradually eased and the pale moonlight that now bathed the glen revealed nothing out of the ordinary; even the mountains, to his critical eye, looked much the same as usual. He shook himself and calling himself all sorts of a fool, made his way down to the road. It was there that he found the landslide; a huge tumble of stone, rock and earth that had spilled over the tarmac and tumbled into the burn. Not only that, it had brought down his only link with the outside world. He lifted his eyes and scanned the scene. The entire line of telephone poles that marched the length of the valley now listed at a crazy angle and several were down — uprooted and splayed across the ground in a tangle of wire, rock and earth. He sighed. There would be work for him aplenty in the morning for the rubble that dammed the burn would have to be cleared. It was a raging torrent and its waters were already spreading over the rough pasture that fringed the foot of the mountains.

His pace quickened as he neared his house for he could see that his sheep had gathered round it. Indeed, the bulk of his small flock seemed to have sought refuge inside his garden. They crowded round him, baa-ing in frantic welcome as he clambered over his flattened gate and, pushing them gently to one side, made his way up the path. What really worried him was that he had heard no sound from his dogs. He found them cowering in the far corner of their shed and his face creased anxiously as they crept towards him on their bellies, whining pitifully. He knew real fear when he saw it. "Come on, Bess," he said, softly. "Come on, Tessa. You're okay now."

The sheep, he reckoned as he hefted the gate up to act as a barricade, would be safe enough penned in the confines of the garden but, conscious of the fact that the telephone lines were down and that he had no contact with the outside world, he kept the two dogs in his bedroom that night and although he was loath to admit it, it was for his own comfort as much as theirs.

5. Glenmorven

"It's very good of you to offer, Helen," Margaret Grant said, relief colouring her voice. "I know you wouldn't have minded having Lewis to stay for a week but to take on the three of them is absolutely wonderful."

"Nonsense, Margaret," Helen's voice echoed down the telephone line. "Believe me, *you're* doing *me* a favour! Shona's growing up and although she loves the glen, she's missing all her friends." Helen's voice sounded suddenly wistful. "I can understand it, you know. Glenmorven is lovely ... but it *is* the back of beyond." She paused then added, "I hope Neil and Clara won't find it too quiet up here."

"Don't worry about them, Helen. I'm sure they'll love it," Margaret Grant stated positively. "They're real outdoor types."

"And are their mum and dad okay about it?"

"They're really grateful and have asked me to pass on their thanks. Actually, from what they said, things sound rather serious. The children's uncle has been admitted to hospital and is due to have an operation at the end of the week. The news doesn't sound too promising but they're hoping he'll pull through."

"I hope so, too. In the meantime we'll do our best to look after Neil and Clara. Lewis told us about them the last time he was here and they sound like nice kids. Shona's really excited about it. It's brightened her up a lot and she'll have a great time showing them round the glen. I'll pick them up tomorrow morning, shall I?"

"That would be marvellous," Margaret sighed. "I'm so grateful to you. Bob's trip has given me the ideal opportunity to see my aunt and I just *can't* pass it up. She's pretty old and although her letters are cheerful enough, I get the impression that she's feeling her age these days ..."

"Are you sure it's all right?" queried Clara later. "I mean, it's very good of her ..."

"It was her husband, who suggested it," Mrs Grant smiled. "He works for the same company as Bob and had heard that your Uncle David was seriously ill. And when they heard of the problem in Texas ... well, he knew there was no way Bob could get out of going."

"And my great-aunt lives near Houston," Lewis added, "so he knew that mum would want to go, too."

"We feel really bad about it, though," Neil said, looking doubtfully at Lewis. "Wouldn't you have liked a trip to the States as well?"

"No way!" Lewis said. "I'd *much* rather be here. And don't feel bad about staying with the Fergusons either," he added. "I bet they're delighted to have us. Glenmorven's quite isolated and now that Shona's getting older they feel guilty at her being on her own during the holidays. There are only a couple of houses there — and the castle, of course."

"Lewis spent a long weekend with them last month. He had a great time," Mrs Grant assured them, "and you'll be able to do a fair bit of hill-walking."

"Sounds fabulous," Neil said and Clara, too, nodded. It had been a great holiday so far. Exploring Aberdeen and going on the cruise to the Shetlands had been fun and now there was the exciting prospect of a remote glen with a castle in it.

"It's a magic place," Lewis grinned, "and you'll really like Shona. She's in my class at school."

"Isn't it Shona who has the secret passage in her house?" Neil asked, looking suddenly interested. "You were going to take us to visit her anyway, weren't you?"

Lewis nodded. "It's an amazing house. Her dad told me that it was once an old hunting lodge. The Fergusons think the tunnel was built as an escape route from Morven Castle in the days when all the clans were at war with one another."

"Mrs Ferguson says she'll pick you up this afternoon," interrupted his mother. "She's coming into town with somebody called Clarissa."

Lewis grinned. "Clarissa isn't a person, Mum. She's a car."

"A car?" echoed Mrs Grant. "The way she talked about it, I thought ..."

"I know," Lewis nodded, "everyone talks about her as though she's a person." He turned to Neil. "It's a fab car," he said, "an old, red Rolls Royce. The Fergusons say it's so old that it knows its way everywhere and can take you into Aberdeen without you even having to touch the steering wheel!"

Mrs Grant smiled indulgently and looked at her watch. "Well, if you're going to stay with Shona for a week, then you'd better start thinking about packing. I've ironed all the washing you brought back from the Shetlands. Remember to take your anoraks with you as well, though," she warned. "The storms that have been hitting the west coast seem to be on their way here. The weather forecast is awful."

Lewis made a face. "That's all we need," he said.

"Things in the glen have changed a bit since you last stayed with us, Lewis," Helen Ferguson remarked as they bowled westwards along the country road in considerable style. Clarissa might have been old and a bit temperamental at times, but she was a beautiful car and could still turn heads. Her red paintwork gleamed and her leather seats, although frayed in places, were soft and supple. She was well-known in the area, too, and many passing motorists waved and smiled as she purred comfortably along a road that showed tantalizing glimpses of the brown, swollen, flood-waters of the River Dee.

"Things have changed *more* than a bit, Mum," Shona said, somewhat indignantly as she sat up straight in her seat. "The glen's not the same at all!" She was sitting between Neil and Clara in the back and now leant forwards to talk to Lewis. "Do you remember meeting my godfather, Uncle Jamie, when we took you to Morven Castle, Lewis?" she asked.

Lewis turned and nodded.

"Well," she said, dramatically, "he's left!"

Neil and Clara looked at her curiously. Shona was a pretty girl with red hair and sparkling green eyes. They'd liked her at once and she, too, had immediately decided that Lewis's friends looked like fun people to know.

"Lord Robertson's gone to Canada," Mrs Ferguson interrupted. "He left at the end of last month to stay with his son and daughter-in-law."

"I suppose it'll be nice for him to see his grand-children," admitted Shona grudgingly, "but we really miss him. You can say what you like, Mum, but the glen's not the same without him!"

"I don't think he would have gone at all if the Americans hadn't offered him such a fantastic rent," Mrs Ferguson conceded. "Apparently, they wanted to buy the estate outright but he refused point blank."

"It's such a shame," Shona added. "He's quite old, you know, and he's hoping that one day his son will come back and run it. For the shooting and the fishing," she explained.

"Do the Americans have any children?" Clara asked.

Shona shook her head but it was her mother who answered. "No, it isn't a family who've taken the estate. They're a weird lot, actually. Hughie thinks they're some kind of sect. They're all men, you see."

"Hughie lives in the glen," Shona grinned at Clara. "Clarissa is his car. Mum uses it while Dad's at work."

"The trouble is that Hughie could well be right about the Americans," her mother said thoughtfully, following her own train of thought. "And if he is, then I find it quite worrying! After all, it's normal to want to get to know your neighbours, isn't it?"

"Mum's peeved," Shona giggled, "because she hasn't been able to show them any Highland hospitality."

"It's not just that," her mother said. "When Jamie Robertson's there, the estate is always open to everyone in the glen and seeing the gates shut ..." she frowned, "is unfriendly to say the least."

"Just face it, Mum. They're not interested in us at all," Shona said with a grin. "They're all fitness freaks from what I've seen of them. If they're not jogging round the glen, they're climbing Morven."

"Morven?" asked Clara.

"Morven," Shona explained, "is our mountain. It's the first thing I see in the morning when I wake up and the last thing I see at night. I *love* Morven."

"I think you'll find it rather interesting," Lewis said, turning in his seat to look at them, "I know I did." Neil missed the knowing smile that crossed his face but Clara didn't. What, she wondered suspiciously, was so special about Morven?

Clarissa's engine grumbled a bit as she reached the top of a rise and turned into the narrow road that led into the wilds of Glenmorven. Lying between the comfortable sweep of high mountains, it was a beautiful glen, Neil thought. He could understand why Shona loved it so much. A brown stream ran along a valley floor that was dappled in sunlight. "There it is," Shona said, pointing upwards, "the big, high mountain with the steep sides and round top. *That's* Morven! Isn't it fantastic?"

Neil lifted his eyes to the hills and gasped. It *was* incredible but not in the sense she meant. The steep, narrow sides of the towering mountain and its gently rounded summit certainly made it stand out against the other sprawling peaks in the area but it wasn't this that made Neil and Clara look at one another in amazement. Shona, seeing the look of complete surprise on their faces, was pleased at the impact the first sight of Morven had made on them. Lewis, too, grinned as both Neil and Clara looked at him questioningly.

"Thought you'd find it interesting," he said blandly.

They did. Before they'd left Edinburgh, Lewis had phoned them and asked them to wear their firestones. Now they knew why — for the minute Morven had appeared before them they'd felt their firestones turn suddenly heavy round their necks and a sense of magic tingle through them. Neil's face lit up. Morven, it would seem, wasn't just any old mountain. Morven was, very definitely, a magic mountain. Clara smiled and they looked at one another in excitement. All of a sudden this holiday was turning into something else!

It was later in the day, when Mr Ferguson was taking Clarissa back to old Hughie that Shona suggested that they all go with him.

Hughie's cottage was further down the glen, set in a hollow surrounded by trees. It looked a secret place, its tiny windows almost covered by brown thread-like strands of creeper that covered the cottage. Green buds were pushing up here and there, however, with the promise of spring.

"It doesn't look much just now," Shona said as they pushed open the garden gate, "but in summer the whole cottage is covered in greenery."

Banks of snowdrops, crocuses and daffodils swept between the trees towards the side of the house while the back, Shona told them, gave onto the lower slopes of the mountain itself. The front door had a tiny porch and a brass knocker. Hughie, however, had heard the car and opened the door as they walked up the path.

He was quite a short man and looked, thought Clara, like a benevolent gnome. Lewis shook his hand, wondering what the MacLeans would make of Hughie. The cottage certainly seemed to have a magic of its own and, from the penetrating look that Hughie had given him on his first visit with Shona, he'd sensed that the small, bright-eyed man had somehow felt the magic in him. Mind you, he thought, he *had* been wearing the magic ring that Prince Casimir had given him. Not only that, he'd also had a firestone round his neck; a gift from the MacArthurs. And since Hughie's cottage was at the foot of Morven, he reasoned that perhaps it wasn't all that surprising that Hughie recognized magic when he met it.

The cottage was plainly furnished but the kitchen was a comfortable, homely room that ran the length of the back of the house and was obviously his living quarters. It was long and low with a beamed ceiling, loads of armchairs and settees, a vast kitchen table and an enormous open fireplace where huge logs crackled and spat. A delicious smell permeated the room for Hughie had been baking.

"You're just in time for tea," he said with a smile, indicating the tray of little cakes, fresh from the oven.

They sat round the old wooden table and although the orange juice was fresh and the cakes delicious, it was the view from the long, low stretch of the kitchen windows that took their breath away. Hughie's back garden had no wall and his land merged with the slopes of Morven itself. Neil and Clara barely heard the conversation between Hughie and Ian Ferguson, so absorbed were they in the view. Clara peered upwards at the mountain; towering high and mysterious over the charming little cottage that nestled snuggly in its gentle hollow. Her eyes sparkled. The cottage, like the mountain, was magic. She was sure of that. Her eyes met those of Neil and Lewis and she knew they felt the same. There was magic here.

6. Malfior's mischief

Prince Kalman stopped at the head of the glen and surveyed it critically. It was a bleak, inhospitable place, he thought disdainfully as he picked his way along a deer path that ran along the side of its barren mountain slopes. Well named, too, he thought sourly — Hell's Glen, the home of the Cri'achan; the stone giants of the north. He shrugged. As far as he was concerned, they were more than welcome to it.

Although the glen was isolated and there was no one to see him, he had nevertheless been wary. The strange attack on the witches' palace had made him careful and since then he had trusted no one; which was why he had merged with a fine stag earlier that morning. The beast was uneasy, though. Although he controlled its mind and its movements, he had immediately sensed that it was fearful and unwilling to enter the glen. It was only when he rounded a jutting spur of rock, however, that he realized why — for walking with great lumbering steps beside the dark stream that ran along the bottom of the valley, were two stone giants. The stag froze in its tracks as a dreadful fear gripped it.

Kalman held the stag firmly in check as it started to panic whilst staring at the massive, rocky figures in utter disbelief, quite unable to believe his eyes. In the world of magic, this was absolutely unheard of! For as long as he could remember, the stone giants had been forbidden to move out of the mountains. It didn't matter that the glen was uninhabited; the spell that Firestar held over them kept them firmly imprisoned. Even he, with the power of the Sultan's Crown behind him, had only half managed to release his friend, Cri'achan Mòr, the King of the Stone Giants, from the mountainside the previous year when he'd asked him to chase Neil and Clara. He frowned as he thought of the two children. Had they not been riding flying horses at the time, they'd never have escaped.

But now this! Stone giants walking through Hell's Glen! It just wasn't possible! For the hundredth time since the assault on the Snow Queen's palace, he wondered what on earth was going on in the world of magic. He had hoped that Cri'achan Mòr would be able to tell him and, he thought agitatedly, with stone giants wandering the glen, it certainly looked as though he might.

"Are you *sure* it's Prince Kalman inside the beast?" Cri'achan Mòr demanded.

Lord Jezail winced at the roaring growl that was the giant's voice. He nodded, turning the eye of the crystal to watch the stag as it picked its way unwillingly into the glen. "I've been tracking him for some time," he said, hiding his irritation. "It's Kalman all right — and I think he's just seen your giants," he remarked with a sour smile.

"Ha!" roared the King of the Giants loudly, waving a massive arm, "that will have given him something to think about!" His rocky face twisted in an evil grin. "Just wait till he arrives! The first

of the Lords of the North to feel my fury! I'm going
to enjoy this!"

The magician turned to the other occupant of
the rocky chamber and raised his eyebrows. He
knew perfectly well that his aide, Count Vassili,
didn't approve of this, his latest venture, but
surely he could see that despite the drastic start,
when they'd all been struck down by the force
of the satellite hitting Firestar, that it was now
starting to pay dividends? A secret smile curved
his thin lips. So far, Malfior had exceeded all his
expectations and, by releasing the giants from the
spell that had held them captive for centuries, he
had shown the Cri'achan the awesome strength of
his new power.

Count Vassili saw his smile and although his
face remained impassive, his thoughts were in turmoil. Lord Jezail, he knew, had great powers but
the very thought of his interfering with Firestar
had frightened the wits out of him. Indeed, when
the force had hit him, the thought had crossed
his mind that his master had managed to kill
off the entire world of magic at a single stroke.
Nevertheless, he had to admit, he seemed to have
somehow pulled it off. Malfior was in place and it
looked as though Lord Jezail would succeed in his
plan to evict the Lords of the North and rule the
world of magic from their glorious halls in Morven.
He smiled a trifle ruefully, for, of the two, he'd far
rather have the Lords of the North in power than
his somewhat bizarre and eccentric master!

"You were right to complain to me," Lord Jezail
was saying to Cri'achan Mòr. "The Lords of the

North were always an idle lot and, quite frankly, they haven't done a proper job for centuries."

"They've really let things slide," agreed the giant.

Lord Jezail nodded understandingly. "There are many others in the world of magic who feel the same as you do, Cri'achan Mòr," he said, in a voice of deep respect, "the trolls, the efrites, the goblins, the people of the trees and the stones."

"All we want are things to be as they used to be," said the giant, emboldened by such praise. His voice deepened at the thought of times past when giants had walked the mountains and the people of the trees in the green wood had been worshipped. "We want to feel the old excitement again when humans feared us and made us offerings and sacrifices."

"And you will, Cri'achan Mòr," Lord Jezail spoke dramatically. "One day soon, you will stand at my right hand in the Halls of Morven. Together we will rule!" His black eyes met those of Count Vassili sharply and recalling his part in such affairs of state, Vassili bowed in agreement. He knew quite well that once Morven was taken, his master would reverse the spell and send the giants back to their prison in Hell's Glen. The very thought was ludicrous. Giants! In the elegant halls of Morven! No way!

"Prince Kalman," the giant growled, glancing at the crystal. "Look, he's demerged from the stag. He's going to hex himself inside the mountain."

"So he is," Lord Jezail muttered. "Well, well! This ought to be interesting!" He glanced quickly

at Vassily and as Cri'achan Mòr turned to enter
his Great Hall to receive the prince, he stepped
into his back, merging with him without the giant
being aware of it.

Demerging quietly from the stag, Prince Kalman
calmed it gently and murmured the words of a hex
that would keep it safe from the giants and ready
for him should he have to leave the mountain in a
hurry. As well might be the case, he thought, suddenly sombre; for the stone giants were no friends
of the Lords of the North and only tolerated him
because he had been cast out of Morven.

His gaze, therefore, was frowning, thoughtful
and decidedly worried as he turned to the barren
slope beside him and, lifting his hands, muttered
the words of a hex that transported him instantly
into the caverns inside the mountain, the home of
Cri'achan Mòr, King of the Stone Giants.

There were caverns and caverns, thought
Kalman, and this one bore little resemblance to
either the elegance of the witches' ice palace or
the rich grandeur of the MacArthurs' halls under
Arthur's Seat. By any standards it was pretty
basic; giants being a fairly primitive lot. Massive
pillars cut from the mountain held aloft a cavern
of roughly-cut walls and ceilings that boasted no
decoration whatsoever. Its floor was covered in
dust and the scatter of boulders in odd corners
said little for their housekeeping. As for the giants
themselves, he eyed them critically, for they talked
in growling roars and, one way or another, were
pretty uncouth.

Cri'achan Mòr sat at one end of the hall on an immense throne hewn out of the side of the mountain itself and looked up as the prince materialized in the middle of his court. A huge giant stepped forward as Kalman appeared and recognizing him immediately, announced him in growling tones.

"Prince Kalman Meriden of Ardray."

Cri'achan Mòr beckoned him forward and the other giants started to talk excitedly amongst themselves as they turned to view their unexpected visitor.

"Cri'achan Mòr!" Prince Kalman moved towards him and bowed low, trying not to wince at the growling, grunting roar of the giants' voices.

"And what brings you to Hell's Glen, Prince Kalman?" asked the giant.

No words of welcome, noted the prince, his senses alert — and not an altogether friendly tone of voice, either.

The other giants in the cavern now moved towards him and despite himself, he found their behaviour unnerving although he knew that the great boulders they were rolling towards him were their equivalent of chairs. As they perched round him, their great legs the size of tree trunks and their eyeless faces gazing at him intently, he took a rather deeper breath than normal before starting his tale. He told them of the attack on himself and the witches and ended by asking if they, themselves, had gone through the same dreadful experience.

The sudden silence that fell as he finished, spoke volumes. He kept his face impassive, however, as he looked round the hall enquiringly. The Cri'achan looked at one another and then at him and said nothing. Kalman didn't often feel fear but as the silence lengthened, the hair on the back of his neck rose as it dawned upon him that, whatever had happened, his friends, the Cri'achan, were friends no more.

"Have you not been to Morven, Prince Kalman?" asked Cri'achan Mòr.

Kalman frowned angrily. "You know perfectly well that I am banned from the mountain," he said haughtily.

Inside Cri'achan Mòr, Lord Jezail picked up on this interesting piece of information. So Prince Kalman had fallen out with the Lords of the North, had he? Even better! That made him vulnerable and alone.

"Then you will not have heard of the attack on Firestar?"

Kalman paled and his head jerked in shock. So *that* was what had happened. It hadn't been a hex at all. It had been an attack on Firestar! Things were worse than he'd thought. Much worse.

"Firestar," he repeated, "then ... then *you* must have felt the attack, too?"

"We did," Cri'achan Mòr acknowledged, "but that is over now. For us, at least!" he added with a dreadful smile. The horrible roar of noise that greeted this remark was, the prince realized, the giants' version of laughter.

"Who attacked Firestar?" he persevered. "Do you know?"

"Oh yes, we know," Cri'achan Mòr laughed

aloud and the giants again joined in. "*We* know,"
he leered slyly and his voice lowered, "but nobody
else does."

"Won't you tell me?"

"Shall I tell him, then?" Cri'achan Mòr asked,
looking round at the assembled giants. "Shall I tell
Prince Kalman?"

Kalman caught the inflection on his name and
clenching his fists, prepared for the worst.

The giants gave a growling roar of triumph. The
King of the Cri'achan leant forward triumphantly
but it was Lord Jezail who spoke through him.
"Listen carefully, *Prince* Kalman," he said in the
ugly rumbling roar of the giants, "*I* now have a
friend in Morven. A friend that is more powerful than Firestar and hidden from it. Its name is
Malfior and one day it will be all powerful. It has
already given the giants their freedom and the
strength to rise from the mountains. And as *it*
grows stronger, so will *I*."

"Really?" Kalman spoke politely but allowed a
distinct trace of disbelief to colour his voice. "And
how did this happen?"

"It came from the sky and attacked Firestar. It
has hidden itself inside it and is gradually eating
its heart out. Quietly, bit by bit, so that Firestar
will never suspect that it is there until it is too
late. Firestar is already weak, for it was Malfior
that released the giants from its spell. Believe me,
Prince Kalman ... Malfior will triumph."

Kalman turned white. He knew perfectly well
that if Firestar were replaced by this evil entity,
Malfior, the world of magic would suffer horribly.

"You're talking nonsense," he said abruptly, "this is a faery story you're telling me, Cri'achan Mòr!"

Cri'achan Mòr shook his head. "My words are true," Jezail said so forcefully that Kalman believed him. "Malfior talks to me and tells me everything that's going on. Believe me when I say that Firestar's days in Morven are numbered."

Cri'achan Mòr's face changed to one of fury. Deprived of speech, he realized that Jezail must have merged with him when his back was turned and there was a distinct pause as he struggled desperately to control the conversation. With a huge effort, he pushed Jezail out of his mind, his stony face grimacing horribly as he did so — after all, this was supposed to be *his* moment of triumph, *his* show of power ... and Jezail had totally ruined it.

"Malfior," he grated furiously, "wishes us to live with him in Morven. The Court of the Lords of the North will be ours and we will rule Scotland and walk its mountains as we did in ancient times. The Cri'achan are rising, Prince Kalman, and we will take Morven!"

The prince frowned but, although he noticed the difference in speech and tone of voice, it was the sense of the words that registered.

"Why are you telling me all this?" he asked sharply.

The ensuing silence told him all that he wanted to know and seeing a piercing yellow light suddenly shine from the stone face, he felt the power of Jezail's magic even as the spell he had cast, hexed him out of the mountain and back into the

body of the great stag that he had left only minutes previously.

Malfior, thought Kalman, was every bit as powerful as Cri'achan Mòr had said for, as the stag
leapt away over the slopes of the mountain, his
heart sank to the pit of his stomach as he realized that in the few seconds that the yellow beam
had focused on him, most of his magic power had
drained away.

His mind reeled from the shock of it all as he
realized that he was now weak, helpless and totally
dependent on the stag.

7. The ghosts of Morven Castle

Tall, turreted and elegant, Morven Castle had, in times past, stood up bravely to the onslaught inflicted by warring clans. Over the years, however, the weather had also taken its toll and, like many of the other old houses and cottages of the glen, the castle was now showing signs of wear and tear. Nevertheless, thought Chuck appreciatively as he walked towards it in the gathering dusk, it retained an elegance rarely found in modern buildings. He drew his jacket more closely round him for although it was April, the wind was bitterly cold. He turned as he reached the cavernous front door that gave onto the main reception hall and, pausing with his hand on the huge handle, looked again at the towering peak that was Morven.

Although he had been pleasantly surprised at the gentle, comforting sweep of Glenmorven, a feeling of acute depression swept over him at the sight of the mountain. He pressed his lips together in sheer frustration as his eyes scanned its steep slopes. There was nothing for it, he reckoned. He was just going to have to wait until Powerprobe locked onto Morven again before he made his next move — aliens or no aliens! For the truth was, he thought disappointedly, that neither he nor any of the geologists and climbers, had discovered anything. He just couldn't believe it. They had been over the mountain again and again with the proverbial fine toothcomb and in all the time they'd been there they hadn't found a thing that was suspicious. The Geiger counter readings were normal, the rocks were normal, the mountain itself was normal; in short, there was absolutely nothing to account for Powerprobe's massive reaction.

The only thing that wasn't normal, as far as he was concerned, was the castle itself for although things had initially gone quite smoothly there had been several strange incidents of late that had made him wonder if the building *was,* actually, haunted. He hadn't believed Lord Robertson when he'd hinted at it but, he reflected, the castle was certainly old enough to house a few ghosts.

He entered the Great Hall and relaxed imperceptibly as his eyes swept over a relatively homely scene. By common consent, they'd made the hall both their living and working area. A long, mahogany table and a dozen chairs had been moved in from the cold vastness of the dining room and a collection of sofas and armchairs, drawn from various parts of the castle, now clustered round the huge fireplace that dominated the hall. A fire had been lit and the logs burned and crackled, sending a welcoming wave of heat through the huge room whose high, panelled walls were hung with a variety of shields, spears, ferocious looking claymores and the odd blunderbuss. As castles went, he thought, it was proving to be remarkably cosy.

Seated round the huge table in the middle of the hall were the group of young men that Mrs Ferguson had objected to so vehemently. Although they looked a pretty motley crew they were, he knew, professional to the core and it was here, he thought as he shrugged off his heavy, padded jacket and slung it over an antique coat stand, that the trouble lay. They didn't believe in ghosts and the unexpected advent of the supernatural had given them the jitters.

"Hi, Chuck," a murmur of greeting ran round a table that was piled high with a variety of dishes. Chuck took his place beside Shane and as they all started eating, the conversation inevitably turned to the strange events of the past few days.

Sam started it. Young and impressionable, he added a lavish amount of ketchup to an enormous hamburger, replaced the sauce bottle and, fitting the top half of the bun in place, looked across the table at Jake. "I don't care what you say, Jake," he said, preparing to take a mouthful, "but *I* reckon the place is haunted."

Jake frowned. "You're not serious, are you?"

"How else do you account for it, then?"

"You slipped on the stairs."

"I didn't slip," Sam protested vigorously. "I tell you, I was pushed!"

"Nobody pushed you, Sammy. I saw you on the stairs and there was nobody anywhere near you!"

"That's what I mean," Sam said irritably. "It must have been a ghost. *And* I felt cold all over. That's what happens in haunted houses. I saw it on a TV programme. There's always a cold feeling around."

"What do you expect?" scoffed Jake. "Castles are draughty places ... all the rooms are huge for a start."

Chuck frowned slightly but made no comment for he, too, on occasion had felt sudden waves of freezing cold air sweep over him for no apparent reason.

Shane's tone of voice was indulgent. "Re-lax," he grinned. "Y'all are going to be plenty warm enough tonight."

Chuck, who had asked for fires to be lit in all the bedrooms, made a mental note of the mockery in his voice and curbed his irritation with an effort. He'd done his best to like Shane but was finding him hard going.

"I agree with Sammy," another geologist said, looking up from his plate and glancing suspiciously round the hall. "I think there *are* ghosts. This castle's old enough to have hundreds."

"Ghosts don't exist, Steve," Jake said, glancing round the table of half-excited, half-fearful faces, "and if one of them dares come into my bedroom, well, I reckon I'll just take one of those blunderbusses from the wall and pump it chock full of lead."

"No, you won't," Chuck interrupted, sternly, "firstly, because I don't want us to be landed with bills for bullet holes in the panelling and, secondly, just in case you've forgotten — ghosts happen to be dead already."

Chuck, nevertheless, was worried, for he himself had had an alarming experience that he hadn't mentioned to the others. The castle was large and, not unnaturally, full of unexpected flights of stairs, odd hallways and long corridors. Despite this, it hadn't taken them long to find their way around, so Chuck hadn't been unduly worried when he'd suddenly found himself in an unfamiliar corridor.

Retracing his steps had proved fruitless and only made him more confused. In the end, however, the experience had a nightmare quality that sent his brain into overdrive; staircases led nowhere, corridors stretched endlessly and, when he turned to look back, he found that he'd passed doors that he didn't even remember seeing. And then, to his relief, he'd heard voices and recognized a familiar flight of stairs. Shane had made no comment when he'd come clattering down the stairs at a run but Chuck knew he'd been curious for he hadn't been able to hide his anxiety or the look of relief that had swept over his face as he'd seen them in the hall.

Later that evening, as he crouched on the patterned Persian carpet in front of the roaring blaze, prodding the logs tentatively with a poker, Shane looked speculatively at Chuck, who was leaning back thoughtfully in a very old armchair of enormous proportions. "So everything that's been happening has a reasonable explanation, then, has it?" he enquired calmly as they all sat round the fire.

"Of course, it has, Shane," Chuck answered, trying to raise a smile. "Surely educated people like us don't believe in ghosts in principle?"

And, as though someone had been listening to every word that had been said, a sudden wave of icy-cold air swept over them. Despite the heat from the blazing fire, it left them staring at one another, their teeth chattering like castanets.

8. The Cri'achan

Sir James Erskine sat up so abruptly that the rest of the committee looked at him in surprise. "Sorry," he apologized, colouring slightly, "I ... er, didn't quite catch what you said, Alex."

Pale April sunlight streamed through the windows of the Scottish Parliament building at the foot of the Royal Mile in Edinburgh and slanted across a small room where five men sat round a polished table that was littered with maps and documents.

Alex Crawford looked across at him and smiled. "I know it sounds ridiculous," he said, looking again at the letter he'd picked out from the sheaf of papers that lay in front of him, "but that's what it says here. Apparently a crofter reported seeing a stone giant walking down the side of a mountain."

"Was he sober?" Duncan Fletcher asked, amid laughter.

"It would seem so," Alex allowed. "There was a storm at the time and he saw it in the lightning flashes. He says it was the size of a house."

"Where was this?" queried Sir James.

Alex looked at the address. "Sutherland," he said, "that's in your constituency Malcolm, isn't it?"

Malcolm MacLeod looked up and nodded. "Stone giants, eh! Well, well! The last time I heard of *them* was in story books when I was a wee lad."

"Did anyone else see it?" Duncan asked. "I mean to say, stone giants the size of houses must be pretty noticeable."

"It's a lonely glen. There *is* another house there but apparently the people in it were all fast asleep at the time."

"And where did it go?"

"According to the letter, it seemed to disappear. He only glimpsed it for a second or so, but by the time he got down to the road, it was gone. The storm had caused a landslide, though, and blocked the road completely. Not only that, it broke a bridge, dammed a river and took down the telephone line as well."

"Have they cleared it yet?"

"I don't think so. It's a pretty isolated area and not very high on anyone's list of priorities. By my reckoning, there are at least fifty glens currently cut off by landslides, broken bridges and the like. The storms have been playing havoc all over the Highlands and it's causing real problems!"

"Climate change?" offered one of the committee members.

"It would seem so. At the moment we're inundated with demands for support from community centres across the Highlands. There are so many people in need of temporary housing that they just can't cope." He sat back in his chair. "You've all seen the media coverage. It's a serious situation. People are having to sleep in schools, libraries and town halls all over the north."

"Do we have a map of the damaged areas?" queried Sir James. "I'd be interested to see it."

"I'll put it up on the screen. Hang on a minute."

Several of the men pushed their chairs back to get a better view as a map of the Highlands clicked up on a wall-mounted screen. It was dotted here and there with red crosses.

"The red crosses mark the glens that have been cut off by landslides," he said, "and you can see just by looking at it, that the damage is widespread."

"Are the crosses just a general indication of damage in the area or do they actually pin-point the landslides?" Sir James asked.

"They pin-point the landslides," was the reply.

"I don't know if it's by accident or design," Malcolm pointed out, "but don't you find it interesting that the landslides seem to be quite ... strategically placed?"

There was silence as five pairs of eyes scanned the map thoroughly.

"You're right, you know, Malcolm," Alex Crawford said slowly. "I didn't think of it like that before, but you're right."

"It surely can't be deliberate ... can it?" someone asked.

"What are you implying?" Duncan frowned. "Landslides don't fall to order ... they're a natural occurrence. There's no rhyme or reason to them."

"The fact is, though," Sir James said, "that each and every one of those landslides blocks a road or breaks a bridge at a vital point. That's why people are having to leave their homes and stay with relatives and friends — because they can't get in or out of their own glens. And in most cases, the phone lines are down as well."

"They could use mobiles, surely?"

Malcolm smiled ruefully. "You're a Lowlander, Duncan. If you'd lived in the Highlands for any length of time, you'd know that quite a lot of people don't have television sets, far less mobile phones. The mountains block out any signal there is."

"It might be my imagination," Alex said, taking charge of the conversation, "but if you look at the crosses, you can see that there's a sort of eastward trend. There are lots of crosses in the north and west but very few in the east."

"That's true," agreed Malcolm. "You can almost tell which glens will be cut off next."

"Another thing is that so far no one has been hurt, no houses have been damaged and as far as I know, no livestock has been killed."

"Yes, it is strange, isn't it? The only damage so far seems to be to the roads, bridges and telephone lines."

"Do you think the landslides are being caused by explosions, then?" Duncan said worriedly. "I mean, if they're being triggered deliberately then the storms would provide good cover. Thunder would disguise the noise of any explosion and nobody would be any the wiser."

"But why would anyone want to do a thing like that?"

"Well, there are so many weirdos around these days, you just never know." He gestured vaguely. "It could be some maniac that wants to restore the Highlands to their natural state."

"That's not as far-fetched as it sounds," Sir

James said thoughtfully, indicating the papers in front of him, "for that's actually what's happening. Look at the statistics we've been given on the numbers of refugees that have moved to coastal areas. To a great extent, the Highlands are being cleared of people!"

Alex Crawford looked at the crosses on the map and regarded Sir James with alarm. "Good heavens," he said, "you could be right, at that!"

"Havers," one of the men snorted. "I just can't believe that people are going round causing landslides all over the place. They'd be spotted for a start! Strangers in the Highlands stand out like sore thumbs, especially shady looking characters!" He leant back in his chair and looked round the table. "There's still the odd bit of cattle rustling that goes on from time to time and the farmers are wary. Besides which, mining the hillside so that roads and bridges are blocked wouldn't only take a lot of skill — it'd need unbelievable luck!"

"It's much more likely to be the Cri'achan," agreed Malcolm MacLeod with a laugh.

"The who?"

"The Cri'achan," Malcolm repeated, "the stone giants."

"You must be joking!"

"That fellow in Sutherland said he saw one ..." Malcolm said reasonably.

"Faery tales!" snorted Duncan.

"Come, now. Haven't you ever heard of the Old Man of the Mountains?"

"Well, yes, vaguely ..."

"He was King of the Cri'achan, the stone giants,"

Malcolm explained. "The story goes that they walked the Highlands for hundreds of years until they tired and when they slept, the mountains captured them, covered them with soil and rocks and made them part of themselves. But legend has always had it that the Cri'achan are still there, asleep on the slopes of the glens and that one day they'll wake and walk the mountains again."

"And you think that one of them has woken up?"

"More than one, by the sound of things," Malcolm said.

"This is altogether ridiculous!" Duncan said loudly. "I can't believe that we're all sitting here listening to such a load of old ... er ... nonsense. I don't believe a word of it! Stone giants! Whatever next, for goodness sake!"

Many of those around the table looked doubtful and the chairman, too, shook his head in disbelief.

"I don't know," Sir James said, "crofters are generally a pretty hard-headed lot. I think he definitely saw something. Maybe it wasn't really a stone giant but it could have been an accident of the weather that loosened the side of a hill and made him think there was one."

"You're probably right, James," Malcolm admitted, "and, really, I was only joking about the Cri'achan."

"Let's keep it that way," the chairman said brusquely. "If the press gets wind of stone giants tramping through the Highlands, there would be panic everywhere!" There was a nodding of heads. "And can you imagine the media?" he added. "They'd milk a story like that for all it was worth!"

"What was the name you gave them, again? The stone giants, I mean?" asked Sir James.

"The stone giants?" Malcolm repeated. "In the Highlands, we call them the Cri'achan."

9. Magic circles

In a cavern, deep inside Arthur's Seat in Edinburgh, the MacArthur sat worriedly on his ornately carved throne. Archie, Jaikie and Hamish sat around him on divans while Arthur, their dragon, lay half-asleep beside them, his head resting on a cushion. The MacArthur stretched wearily, drawing his fur-lined cloak around him. Its deep red velvet was worn in places but it was comfortable and kept off the chill. Most of the day had been spent discussing the problem of Firestar and his mind was still going round in endless circles as he pondered the dangers of another attack.

Looking up as Arthur lifted his great head and exhaled a long breath of fire and smoke, the MacArthur straightened and rose to his feet. A magic carpet had just sailed into the Great Hall and he raised his eyebrows as he saw that it carried Sir James.

"Give over, Arthur," Archie said excitedly as he sprang to his feet, waving away the clouds of smoke, "you don't want to choke our visitor, do you?"

Sir James smiled as he looked round the Great Hall, his eyes taking in the huge, red dragon and a few clustered groups of MacArthurs who stared up at him as he swooped by. It was a comfortingly familiar sight and as breathtakingly magnificent as ever. He smiled at Hamish and Jaikie as they helped him off the carpet and walked over to the

raised dais that held the MacArthur's throne.
Eyeing him shrewdly as he bowed low, he wondered what had happened to put the MacArthur
out of temper. Or perhaps he's been ill, he thought,
for gleaming under the fur of his robe he glimpsed
a heavy necklace of firestones; powerful, magic
stones which protect their wearer from harm.
So, he noticed were Archie, Hamish and Jaikie.
Something must have happened, he decided, for
despite their many hair-raising adventures, he had
never seen the MacArthur look quite so drawn and
haggard.

Hamish and Jaikie pulled up a divan for him and
once Arthur had settled his great bulk comfortably, with Archie sitting cross-legged beside him, Sir
James poured out his tale about the Cri'achan.

"The rest of the committee laughed it off," he
explained. "They just didn't believe the crofter's
story. But I did. I remember Neil and Clara telling me how they were chased by the Old Man of
the Mountains when they were on their way to
Inveraray last year — and he was a stone giant,
wasn't he? Must have been, for Clara saw him."

The MacArthur listened to Sir James carefully.
"We heard that the Cri'achan are walking the
mountains again," he said worriedly, "but from
what you say, it sounds as though they're still very
weak. They can grow a lot taller than a house, you
know. But you've got one thing wrong, James; the
stone giants aren't causing the landslides, they *are*
the landslides!"

"What do you mean?"

"I told you. The giants must still be weak. They

have the strength to rise from the slopes of the mountains but from what you say, they can't walk far before they collapse — and that's your land-slide."

Sir James turned white for, unlike them, he had all the facts and figures at his fingertips. "But if that's true," he said slowly, "they must have intel-ligence of a sort. Look here," he pointed at his map, "and here and here; all the landslides are in strategic positions that close the glens to traffic. They've covered roads, bridges and railway lines and they're moving steadily eastwards. No one's been hurt yet but ..."

"No one will be hurt, Sir James," the MacArthur assured him, "the stone giants aren't vicious. They're only dangerous because of their size. All they want is space to move around the moun-tains."

"Well, they're succeeding. People are having to leave their homes, you know. It's no joke! The Highlands are being emptied."

It was only when he looked closely at the posi-tions of the landslides on the map, however, that the MacArthur's face altered and he gave a hiss of alarm. Jaikie and Hamish looked puzzled until the MacArthur drew his finger towards Aberdeen.

"Morven," Jaikie said in alarm. "You don't think ..."

"If the Cri'achan are heading for Morven then things could get out of hand," the MacArthur said grimly, slapping his knee, "as if we didn't have enough on our minds already!"

Sir James's eyes flew from face to face as he

sensed their concern. Things were obviously far more serious than he'd thought. "Something else has happened, hasn't it?" he ventured.

Looking at Sir James's worried face, the MacArthur nodded, wondering if it was fair to burden him with another, more serious, problem. He sighed and began his tale. By the time he had told him of Morven, the existence of Firestar and the dreadful attack that had almost killed them all, Sir James was sitting bolt upright. Now he knew why the MacArthur looked a couple of hundred years older than usual.

"When did all this happen?" he asked.

"About a month ago."

"And you say the Rumblewhatsit, the hobgoblin, saw a man on the monitor?"

The MacArthur nodded. "What really worries us is that there could be another attack at any time. That's why we're wearing firestones. The danger is that if it lasts for longer, we ... well, we just mightn't be so lucky. It came out of the blue, you know. No warning at all!"

Arthur, with an eye on Archie, blew a very small cloud of smoke in agreement.

"And this ball of energy that you call Firestar? I mean ... is it all right now?"

The MacArthur nodded. "Yes," he answered. "The hobgoblins were worried about it at first but they can sense its moods and thoughts and they'd know if it had been injured. We'd all know," he added frankly, "for Firestar is reflected in all of us."

"What about the Sultan?" Sir James asked. "Was

he affected? And Lord Rothlan? Prince Casimir?
And your daughter, Lady Ellan?"

"They all felt it," the MacArthur said gravely.

"Have you talked about it with them?"

"We had a meeting in Morven with the Lords
of the North," the MacArthur said gravely. "A few
decided not to come — Lord Jezail declined and
quite frankly he wasn't missed.

"Lord Jezail?" queried Sir James. "I don't think
I've heard you mention him before?"

The MacArthur pursed his lips disapprovingly.
"To tell you the truth," he said frankly, "very few
people like the man. He lives in Ashgar."

"Ashgar? Where on earth's that?"

The MacArthur raised his eyebrows. "Haven't
you heard of it? It's one of those small principali-
ties tucked away in Central Europe ..."

Sir James shook his head. "My geography of
Central Europe isn't all that brilliant," he confessed.

"It's on the fringes of Asia and quite close to
Turkey. I've never been there but Prince Casimir
and Prince Kalman used to stop over in Ashgar on
their way to Turkey to buy magic carpets."

"In the days before the Sultan's crown was stolen," Archie added.

"Ah, yes! The Sultan! Did he come?"

"He came by magic mirror," the MacArthur
nodded, "and ended up chairing the meeting. He's
a forceful character and ... well, the Lords of the
North are very old and a bit dithery nowadays.
They were quite happy to hand the meeting over
to him. Lord Rothlan and Prince Casimir were

there, of course and we talked for hours but in the end, nothing was resolved. We couldn't find out what the force was but we think it may have come from the sky — like a bolt of lightning or something. The only thing we know for sure is that it wasn't an attack by a stray magician. It was a man that Rumblegudgeon saw on the screen."

"I presume you've put a protective shield round Morven?"

"It was the first thing we did," nodded the MacArthur.

Sir James sat back. "This is serious," he muttered, "but there are some clues. You should have told me about this before, you know. If the hobgoblin saw a man on the screen and you think the attack came from the sky, then the chances are that maybe some sort of spacecraft is involved." He saw their blank looks. "You know," he gestured vaguely, "... spaceships, satellites and the like ... Machines in space that circle the earth and transmit data about all sorts of things. Lots of countries have them — America, Russia and France to name but a few."

There was a silence.

"America?" Hamish looked at Jaikie, his eyes startled.

Jaikie sighed. "You'd better tell Sir James about the Americans at Morven Castle, MacArthur."

"Morven Castle?" Sir James repeated.

"It's in Glenmorven," Hamish explained, "and quite close to the mountain."

"There are four or five of them," the MacArthur admitted. "Young chaps, all of them. They leased the castle from Lord Robertson not long after Firestar was attacked and since they arrived they've done nothing but climb all over the mountain. They must know that there's something odd about it for they've taken rock samples and gone over it with some sort of machine as well."

"They have, have they?" said Sir James interestedly.

"They haven't found Firestar, though," Hamish said. "They arrived after we'd put a protective shield round the mountain."

"I'll try and find out who they are and what they're up to, if you like," Sir James offered. "I've a friend in Aberdeen who might be able to help."

Jaikie grinned, despite the gravity of the situation. "No need for that, Sir James. We've got spies in the castle already!"

"Ghosts," nodded the MacArthur.

"Ghosts?" repeated Sir James, looking taken aback.

"Red Rory MacGregor and the Black MacTavish," the MacArthur said, smiling at his expression. "Fearsome fighters, the pair of them. They've haunted the castle for years. They never bother Lord Robertson, of course," he added, "but these Americans have really put their noses out of joint. Apparently, they suspected from the start that something strange was going on and when they heard them talking about how to get into the mountain — well, they passed the message on to the Lords of the North."

"They were talking about blowing a hole in it with explosives," Hamish said disapprovingly.

"How on earth do you know all this?" Sir James asked in amazement.

"The Lords of the North have given them a crystal ball," the MacArthur said reassuringly, "and they keep us up to date on what's going on."

"They're trying to scare the Americans out of the castle at the moment but so far they haven't had much success," Archie added, smiling mischievously. "The trouble is that they're invisible, of course, so their scope, at the moment, is a bit limited. They reckon they might have to materialize if they're going to get any results."

Sir James left the hill every bit as worried as the MacArthur. As his carpet took him up through the blackness of the tunnels inside Arthur's Seat into the watery sunshine of an April day, his mind was busy. As always, the magic carpet became invisible the minute it left the hill and as it soared towards Morningside, heading for his flat, he made a mental note to give Bob Grant a ring. Bob was in Aberdeen. Maybe *he* could find out who the Americans were ...

10. Jelly Beans

The minute Prince Kalman merged back into the body of the stag, the petrified beast took off, covering the slopes of the mountainside in great, flying leaps. It didn't need any urging, for the two giants that had been striding along the bottom of the glen had already turned towards the slopes and were even now lumbering menacingly upwards.

Bounding wildly across the hillside, Kalman thought at one stage that they might yet escape. The giants obviously thought so, too, for they started throwing boulders at them. Their aim, however, was way out and although the huge rocks bounced and crashed around them, they did little damage apart from freaking out the stag, which, by this time, was totally beyond Kalman's control. In a blind panic, it raced across the heather taking dangerously great leaps as it cleared tumbling streams and scattered outcrops of rock. As the giants came ever closer, however, it turned frantically into a broad gully that seemed to offer a way of escape. It turned out to be a trap, however, as on turning a corner, Kalman realized with a sinking heart, that the gully was a dead end.

The giants roared in triumph as they saw that the stag was at their mercy while Kalman, deprived of most of his magic, knew real fear. There was nothing he could do but wait and as the stag reared desperately against the walls of the sheer cliff that barred their way, he watched in an agony of frustration and bitterness as the giants gathered boulders from the slopes. Was this how he was going to end his life?

Had the giants thrown the boulders at them, there and then, they might well have destroyed the prince. Afterwards, he could never quite work out why they hadn't finished him off at once. It might have been that they just didn't know that their new-found strength was limited but they certainly wasted valuable time and energy by gathering together a handy pile of rocks. It proved their undoing for, with sudden grunts of horror, they found themselves literally falling apart. Kalman, looking on in amazement, breathed a sigh of relief as he watched them collapse in front of him. Hope stirred within him and his heart lightened. He hadn't realized that the giants were quite so vulnerable. Maybe things weren't as bad as he'd thought, he mused. It might well be that Cri'achan Mòr had quite a long way to go before he became Lord of Morven.

Although the giants were now no more than a pile of rubble, Prince Kalman waited until the quivering stag had quietened down before he urged it over their broken remains and turned its head towards the north-east and Morven.

Morven! Thoughts of the mountain filled his mind. He just *had* to get there. All thoughts of enmity had fled. The quarrel with his father and the Sultan was nothing compared with this new danger, which posed the most serious threat that the Lords of the North had ever had to face. Could this Malfior be destroyed? he wondered. It was cer-

tainly a powerful force, for the amount of magic
that he had been left with was pitifully small ...
nothing like the strength of power he was used
to. Despite his weakness, he knew that the Lords
of the North had to be warned at once and he
only hoped that Firestar would be able to deal
with the strange, fearsome entity that lurked in
its depths.

The going, after that, was painfully slow. Kalman
fulminated at their lack of progress for the stag
had to be given time to rest, graze and drink. It
was, however, a powerful animal and between
times, kept a steady pace. Nevertheless, it was well
after midnight when they reached the shores of
Loch Lomond.

The waters of the loch gleamed silver in the
moonlight and it was while Kalman was looking for a place for the stag to rest that the giants
picked up on him again. Cri'achan Mòr must be
tracking him through a crystal, he thought, as a
huge giant rose suddenly, in tearing jerks from the
slopes of the hills and bore down upon him in a
thunder of noise.

Petrified by its abrupt appearance, the stag
slipped and slid its way frantically downhill to
where a road wound its way round the shores of
the loch. Although busy with traffic during the
day, there wasn't a car in sight at this time of
night and the frightened animal, who would not
normally have gone anywhere near a road, feeling the smooth tarmac under its hooves, streaked
along with the giant crashing heavily behind. Keep
going, Prince Kalman urged the stag, willing it to

run faster. Keep going and perhaps it'll run out of energy like the others did.

The giant, however, was gaining and again Kalman thought he was done for when, lights blazing, a huge trailer carrying a load of tree trunks came thundering round a sharp bend in the road. The stag gave a sudden, spectacular leap that cleared the road but the giant was not so fortunate; nor so agile. As the astonished driver slammed on his brakes, the momentum of the trailer sent it straight into the giant's legs. It was what you might call a no-win situation. The giant didn't stand a chance. It broke into hundreds of pieces as its legs were demolished under it and roaring with fury, fell over the trailer in a jumble of rocks, stones and earth.

A van, headlights blazing, drew up with a screech of brakes behind the trailer. Kenny and Larry, sitting in the front seat, had been trying to overtake the monstrous vehicle for miles and its sudden halt took them by surprise and nearly sent them straight into the back of it.

Kalman, surrounded by ferns at the side of the road, looked at the van curiously, through the eyes of the stag. He had never in his life seen anything to equal it, for in the light of its blazing headlights he could see that it had been painted in the weirdest mixture of fluorescent colours that he'd ever had the misfortune to clap eyes on. The two lads that jumped down from the front seats looked around seventeen or eighteen and, colour-wise, weren't actually that much better than their van. Their vivid trousers, horrendous jackets and

fantastically belled hats, however, served to give
Kalman a clue as to their identities. Light dawned!
Jesters, he thought, that's what they must be —
the modern equivalent of jesters! There could be
no other reason for the multi-coloured clothes that
they sported. He eyed their vehicle speculatively
as they rushed to help the driver of the trailer and
gradually deciphered the mosaic of lettering that
shone vividly from its side. *"The Jelly Beans,"* he
read, frowning in puzzled wonder. *Jelly Beans?*

It was actually quite some time before Kenny
and Larry returned. The huge trailer had suffered little or no damage from the collision with
the giant and apart from being shaken, the driver
had recovered quickly enough. Nevertheless, he
had a tight schedule to follow and, anxious to get
on his way, he'd enlisted their help to clear the
stones from the road so that he could continue his
journey.

Kalman, by this time, had decided that the jesters and their van was just what he needed. As the
two colourful figures strode back along the road,
the stag limped forward and collapsed on its knees,
seemingly totally exhausted. It lifted its head
limply and eyed Larry beseechingly as he made to
open the door.

"Hey, Kenny," Larry called to his mate, "there's
a muckle great stag here, by the side of the road!"

Kenny appeared round the side of the van, the
bells on his hat tinkling in the still night air. After
a disaster at the hairdresser's a while back that
had left him looking like a fair-show freak, he'd
decided to wear the multi-coloured hat all the time

— or at least until his hair grew in again. This had proved a good move publicity-wise and although his hair had long since grown, they'd both continued to wear their startling outfits more or less all the time. Needless to say, the Jelly Beans, for that's what they called themselves, were instantly recognizable in most towns and villages up and down the west coast of Scotland.

"That must be the stag that the giant was chasing," he said, for the trailer driver had told him of the fantastic sight that had met his eyes as he took the bend. He walked up to it cautiously, mindful of the broad spread of antlers that topped the stag's head.

"*If* what he said was true," cautioned Larry. "I don't know if he was having us on or not! All those rocks and things — it could have been a landslide."

"I believed him all right," Kenny muttered. "For heaven's sake man, did ye no' hear them talking about giants in the last pub we were in?"

"Aye, but ... that was just talk, wasn't it ...?" Larry gulped and tailed off uncertainly as the huge stag scrambled to its feet and moved towards them. The bells in his fantastic hat jingled as he started back in alarm. "Blimey, Kenny," he whispered, grabbing his arm as he flattened himself against the painted side of the van.

Kenny stiffened as the stag stood quietly in front of them but when it spoke, he eyed Larry sideways and then peered around to see if anyone else was there.

"What was that you said, Kenny?" Larry asked.

"I didn't say anything," Kenny whispered, his voice trembling as he glanced anxiously at the stag.

"Give over, mate," Larry looked at him strangely, "it must have been you! There's ... there's only us here."

"It wasn't me, I tell you! And if it wasn't *you* ... then ... it must have been the stag!"

"I said, I want to go to Ballater," Kalman tried not to sound too impatient.

Kenny gulped and grabbed at Larry's arm. "Did you hear that? It *is* the stag that's talking!" He looked at the animal in utter disbelief, for the words didn't seem to come from the stag's mouth at all; like Larry, he just heard the voice in his head. "You – want – to – go – to – Ballater," he repeated.

The stag nodded its head forcefully. "The giants are chasing me. I must reach Ballater as soon as I can. It's very important."

"Ah dinni believe this," Larry moaned, his face going suddenly grey.

Kalman sighed and using a little more of the magic left to him, kindled their spirit of adventure. It worked. Kenny suddenly grinned at Larry, his eyes shining. "Come on, Larry," he said. "I've no idea what's going on but we've got to save the stag! As far as I'm concerned, we're going to Ballater!"

"Well, I know but ..." Kenny's excitement was infectious and looking at the stag with a new light in his eyes, Larry felt the full force of Kalman's personality. Avoiding the attention of giants and taking a stag to Ballater suddenly seemed the most

sensible thing in the world and forgetting everything in the excitement of the moment, Larry ran
behind the gaudily-painted van and held its back
door open with something of a flourish. "Ballater
it is then," he said, the bells in his cap jingling
wildly, "if you can fit yourself in here, that is!"

11. Confrontation

Despite the bad weather that continued to plague Scotland, Glenmorven was bathed in sunshine when the children woke the next morning and by the time they made their way lazily downstairs for breakfast, Shona's father had already left for work in Aberdeen.

"It's a lovely day," Helen Ferguson said as they sat round the breakfast table by the big window in the kitchen. She picked up a huge jug and poured glasses of orange juice for them as they tucked into scrambled eggs on toast. "Why don't you make the most of it and have a picnic on Morven?"

"Sounds great," Lewis said. Neil and Clara nodded enthusiastically. They were wearing their firestones under their T-shirts and couldn't wait to see what the mountain had to offer.

"Right, that's settled then. I'll make you some sandwiches and you can take apples and bananas from the fruit bowl." She smiled. "I was going to say that it's a bit of a stiff climb but Lewis tells us that you grew up climbing Arthur's Seat so I won't have to give you any advice!"

They left the house and made their way across the road to the rough grassland and the plank bridge that spanned the rushing stream that threaded the foot of the glen.

"The burn's really full, isn't it?" Lewis remarked as they stopped to watch the powerful swirl of brown water as it passed beneath them. "You must have had lots of rain?"

"Heaps," answered Shona, "which is strange, really, for we usually miss out on storms and stuff. My friend Jennifer lives in the next glen and she's always complaining that we seem to have the best of the weather." She looked up at the steep slopes that swept before them. "Mind you, Morven does seem to attract electrical storms from time to time. There was a terrific one a couple of weeks back. It's a pity you missed it for it really was spectacular. There were flashes of lightning on top of the mountain and the thunder was deafening. Hughie says that it's the Gods of the Mountain having a firework display!"

"The Gods of the Mountain?" Neil turned his head sharply to look at her.

"That's what he says," she answered, slightly surprised at his reaction. "There aren't any really, of course."

They had their picnic on a grassy bank on the slopes of Morven. It had been a tough climb as Shona's mother had said and slipping off their backpacks, they relaxed gratefully. The view in front of them was certainly spectacular. Shona pointed out the mountains that lay round them. "Over there," she ended, "just beyond that ridge, is Glen Garchory and Peter's Hill."

"Glen Garchory? That's where Jenni lives, isn't it?" remarked Lewis, shading his eyes with his hand as he peered across the glen. "We visited her the last time I was here," he said, turning to Neil and Clara. "She goes to the same school as we do but she's a year below us."

"We could go and visit her tomorrow if the weather's good," Shona offered, looking round enquiringly. "What do you think?"

"Sounds great," nodded Neil.

"It's a bit of a walk but I told her you were coming and she's looking forward to meeting you."

Hungry after the long climb, they unpacked the food and had spread it out on the grass when Neil noticed movement on the slopes below.

"Don't look round," he said suddenly, "but I think we're going to have visitors."

"Where?" Shona asked, startled. "Who?"

"I can see some men down there climbing up towards us. They look as though they might be the Americans your mum is so anxious to meet!"

"Let's pretend we haven't seen them," Shona said swiftly. "I hope they're not going to bother us."

By the time the Americans arrived, the four children were sprawled out on the grass, drinking orange juice and munching on sandwiches. They looked up, however, as the men sauntered over and although their manner was casual and they were smiling pleasantly, they towered over them somewhat menacingly.

"Hi, there!" said one, who seemed to be their leader.

"Hullo," Shona answered, getting to her feet.

"May I ask who you are, li'l lady?" he drawled. The accent was distinctly American.

Shona's hackles went up. "I might ask you the same thing," she said brusquely. After all, she thought, it was really none of his business who they were.

"Sure," the American said. "My name's Shane and these are some of my buddies." He gestured towards them and they held their hands up in greeting. They seemed friendly enough but Lewis noticed that their smiles didn't reach their eyes.

"Actually," Shona confessed, "I know who you are."

"You do, do you?" The man spoke with a definite drawl.

"Mmmm," nodded Shona, "you must be some of the Americans that have rented Lord Robertson's castle." She held out her hand. "My name's Shona Ferguson and these are my friends; Neil, Clara and Lewis. I live down there in the glen. We've seen you passing it in your 4x4."

Although Shane shook her hand, his expression changed to a frown. "You're right, Miss Ferguson," he said, "we do live at the castle. But we haven't only rented the castle, you know, we've rented the entire estate. This mountain," he gestured vaguely, "is part of it. I'm afraid you're trespassing and I must ask you to leave."

"Leave?" Shona looked taken aback. "I most certainly will not. I've spent my life climbing this mountain."

Shane's expression didn't change and neither did his tone of voice. "I'm really sorry," he said, "but the mountain is private property, Miss. I don't particularly want to spoil your picnic but once you've finished eating, you'll have to go."

Neil had vaguely heard that in Scotland there was no law of trespass. "You can't make us leave, I'm afraid," he said, moving to stand beside Shona, his voice sounding a lot more confident than he felt, "there's no such thing as trespass under Scottish Law."

Good for you, thought Lewis, hiding a grin at the sudden look of indecision that crossed the American's face.

"Besides which," Shona said, her face pink with annoyance, "Lord Robertson is my godfather and I don't think he'd like me to be chucked off Morven. He knows how much I love it." She glared at Shane mutinously.

"We're only having a picnic," Neil said reasonably, turning round and gesturing towards the juice and fruit on the grass. "We're," he choked suddenly and cleared his throat, "... we're not doing any damage or anything." He tried to make his voice casual and, with an effort, kept his eyes firmly fixed on Shane's face, for while they'd been talking, two goat-like little creatures in baggy trousers and short waistcoats had wandered casually onto the grassy slope and were standing nearby, watching them interestedly. Lewis saw them, too, and nudged Clara gently. She looked up and such was her surprise that she gasped audibly.

The men standing beside Shane, however, were not as idle as their casual pose suggested. They saw her face change and immediately followed her gaze. Apart from a few stunted bushes, there was nothing there that they could see but they instinctively moved forward. The hobgoblins, for their part, froze in horror as they realized that all eyes seemed to be trained on them. Then, as their tendrils flared in a sudden frenzy of movement, they grabbed at one another with tiny hands, took two steps backwards, turned and fled on little hooves.

"What were you looking at?" Shane asked, his voice harsh.

Pretending to be frightened, Clara shook her head in alarm. "I ... I thought I saw a snake," she whispered fearfully. Shane looked totally unimpressed, as well he might, so Clara did the only thing she could think off.

Everyone but Neil watched in consternation as she gave a quivering, heart-wrenching sob. Her blue eyes filled with huge tears and, as she fished in her pocket for a tissue, they spilled, unchecked, down her cheeks.

"Now look what you've done!" Lewis said angrily to the Americans as Shona, full of genuine concern, put her arm protectively round Clara. "You've spoiled our day and anyway ... we've almost finished our picnic. We'll be going home soon." Besides which, he thought, an ugly, sharp wind with a cutting edge to it had blown up and black clouds were gathering over the distant peaks. It looked as though they'd be lucky to get back home without being soaked to the skin.

Clara's tears, however, did not deflect the Americans from their purpose. As though responding to a signal, they fanned out casually and made an unobtrusive, but thorough, search of the grassy slope — especially the part that had attracted Clara's attention. In fact, they wandered round for some time until Lewis muttered that he thought they'd better make themselves scarce.

"What on earth are they up to?" Shona said, stuffing uneaten apples into her backpack. "Honestly, how dare they! Wait until I tell my dad! He'll be furious!"

"Are you all right, Clara?" Lewis looked worried as Clara scrubbed at her eyes with a tissue and continued to sob intermittently. "They've moved off now but I think they're still keeping an eye on us."

"She's fine," Neil grinned. "Clara's the only person I know that can cry to order — and, I must say, it has its uses!"

Clara winked at Lewis as she slipped her backpack over her shoulders and, much to his amusement, sniffed miserably as they started down the slope.

"You can give over now, Clara," Neil said when they were finally out of earshot, "they can't hear you any more!"

Lewis looked grim. "That was what you might call a strange encounter," he said meaningfully.

"Very strange," agreed Neil, careful not to say more although his mind was full of what he'd just seen. *What on earth were those strange little creatures and where had they come from?*

"I can't believe that just happened," Shona muttered. "It was really strange the way they searched everywhere as though they were looking for something." She looked at Clara. "Did you really see a snake, Clara?"

Clara sniffed and dabbed at her nose with a tissue to give herself time to think. She couldn't tell Shona she'd seen some kind of faery but she knew she had to say something. "I saw something move," she admitted, "and I thought it might be a snake but there wasn't anything there — it was probably just the wind in the grass."

12. Trouble spots

Prince Casimir pressed his lips together and hung on grimly to his temper. He'd never felt more like shaking Lord Alarid in his life. What, in heaven's name, was wrong with him? He'd readily agreed to go to Morven when the MacArthur had passed on the gist of Sir James's worries, thinking that Alarid would take immediate action against the Cri'achan. The attack on Firestar, however, seemed to have done little more than paralyze his thought processes for try as he might, he was getting nowhere fast.

"The Cri'achan, Lord Alarid," he said again, emphasizing the importance of his words, "must be stopped while they're still weak."

Lord Alarid shook his head. "Let's wait and see what happens, Casimir," he replied, somewhat irritably. "If the giants are as weak as you say then nothing will come of them. They are far from Morven and this strange attack has upset everything."

"The MacArthur is seriously worried about them, milord ..."

Lord Alarid waved his hand. "The MacArthur might be worried, Casimir, but he is far away in Edinburgh. You are here in Morven and can surely feel that Firestar itself isn't the slightest bit concerned." He looked at him shrewdly. "You must feel within yourself that Firestar is aware of what happened and is ready to fight back should there be another attack?" Prince Casimir nodded. The overall sense of well-being that emanated from Firestar gave him confidence, but a niggling doubt persisted that the unknown force might also have upgraded the weapons in its armoury. As far as he was concerned, there was still a chance that Firestar could be seriously damaged.

"If there is another attack then Firestar will, I'm sure, be able to counter it," Alarid looked at him confidently. "Forget about the giants," he said. "I assure you, they pose no danger to us at all."

Feeling totally frustrated, Prince Casimir bowed low and was about to withdraw when Lord Alarid remembered the hobgoblins.

"By the way, you'd better see Rumbletop," he continued. "Some of the hobgoblins were spotted on the hill by those Americans. They're quite upset about it."

"Seen?" repeated Casimir, startled. "How ..."

But by then, Lord Alarid had closed his eyes and with a snort of exasperation, Casimir went downstairs to the machine and found Rumbletop.

"What's been going on, Rumbletop?" he demanded. "Lord Alarid said that some of you were seen on the hill?"

Rumbletop tutted as his tendrils started to grow. "They didn't mean any harm, Prince Casimir," he apologized. "Rumbletumble says they were on their way down to the glen."

"Down to the glen?" queried Casimir. "What on earth for?"

"To see Hughie, milord. He gives them biscuits and honey cakes."

Rumbletop looked relieved as Casimir hid a smile. "Does he now? Hmmm, always was a nice chap, Hughie." He looked at the little hobgoblin through eyes that were unexpectedly kind. "But that doesn't explain how they were seen."

"Shona has friends staying with her. Two boys and a girl. Rumbletumble said it was quite obvious that they could see them."

"Did he hear their names, by any chance?"

"Yes, he did. They're called Neil, Clara and ..." He stopped as Casimir held up his hand.

"Neil, Clara ... and Lewis," finished Prince Casimir with an exasperated sigh. "I might have known!"

Rumbletop looked amazed. "You know them, milord?" he asked.

"You *could* say that," Casimir agreed, a smile hovering about his lips. "So Neil, Clara and Lewis are here in the glen, are they? How interesting! You don't need to worry about them, Rumbletop. They are known to us. They'd be wearing their firestones. That's how they would be able to see Rumbletumble and his friend."

Rumbletop looked gobsmacked. "Firestones," he repeated, startled, "but they're human children, surely?"

Casimir nodded. "May I ask what happened between them and the Americans? Just as a matter of interest."

"They were telling them to get off the mountain, milord. Shona was cross."

"I'm sure she was," Casimir said, smiling at the thought. All the Lords of the North took an interest in the families in the glen and over the years had watched Shona grow up from a toddler to a leggy teenager whose favourite pastime was climbing and scrambling over the slopes of Morven. "And the other three?"

"The girl cried."

At this, Casimir raised his eyebrows in surprise. "Cried?" he queried. "That doesn't sound like the Clara I know."

"The Americans knew she'd seen something. They searched everywhere. She didn't mention us, though. She told them she'd seen a snake, but ... well, I don't think they believed her."

Mr Ferguson, when he heard Shona's story of how they'd been more or less ordered off the mountain, didn't believe Clara's story either. Not that it worried him but somehow she didn't seem the kind of girl who would make up stories about snakes. He turned to Shona. "I hope you weren't rude to them, Shona?"

Shona blushed. "I wasn't rude exactly," she confessed, "but I was really mad. You know how I love Morven."

Her father sighed. "I think I'd better phone the castle and make an appointment to see these Americans," he said, "and you four can come along and apologize at the same time."

"Apologize!" Shona looked startled. "What for? We didn't know we were doing anything wrong!"

"They're our neighbours, Shona," her father said in a voice that brooked no defiance, "and I don't want there to be any bad feeling between us."

"But there's no law against trespassing ... Neil said ..."

"Neil's probably quite right about the law of trespass, Shona, but we have to respect our neighbours' wishes. I think you should stay off the mountain until Jamie Robertson comes back from Canada."

Shona looked totally horrified. "Stay off Morven!" she repeated. "But ... Uncle Jamie's going to be away for months and months."

"I know it's hard, Shona," her mother said comfortingly, "but it's not our land, you know. Jamie's just been kind in letting everyone use it."

"Look at it from the Americans' point of view, Shona," her father pointed out. "They've paid a lot of money to rent the estate and they want it to themselves."

Tears gathered in Shona's eyes. "I know you're right, Dad," she admitted, "but the rest of the year is going to be perfectly foul. And what am I going to do in the summer hols? I spend most of my time on Morven. You know I do!"

"Let your father talk to the Americans first," her mother suggested. "Once we explain the situation and tell them you love the mountain and wouldn't dream of causing any damage then I'm sure they'll change their minds."

But, as it happened, the Americans didn't change their minds. Ian Ferguson looked more than a little annoyed as he put the telephone receiver down and glanced across at his wife.

"They don't seem a very friendly lot, do they?" Helen said, having heard his side of the conversation.

"No, they don't," he admitted. "I spoke to this Shane character that Shona told us about and he was really quite adamant. He didn't want me to visit the castle to talk the matter over, nor did he want the children to come and apologize and as for giving Shona permission to climb the mountain when she pleased ... no way!"

"We've been so used to having Jamie around," his wife frowned, "that we've taken his kindness for granted. Shona said that the glen had changed and she's right. It's not a friendly place any more."

"I think I'll nip over and have a word with Hughie," her husband mused thoughtfully. "He takes a few salmon from the river and the odd stag now and then. I wouldn't like that lot to catch him at it."

"It's hardly likely is it?" Helen frowned.

"You never know," Ian replied, slipping his arms into the sleeves of his jacket, "but I'd better warn him that they're not exactly an obliging lot. Say goodnight to the kids for me, will you. I might be late! You know Hughie; once he starts talking, he can go on for hours!"

Although Hughie didn't talk for hours, he nevertheless had a lot to say and as he listened, Ian Ferguson's face grew more and more puzzled.

"They're a weird lot, Ian," Hughie said grimly, his weather-beaten face anxious. "I don't know what they're here for but whatever it is it's something to do with Morven."

Ian Ferguson ran a hand through his greying hair. "They've been at it ever since they arrived;

taking rock samples, going over it with a Geiger counter ... the lot. They chucked Shona and her friends off it this afternoon," Ian remarked. "Told her she was trespassing. I phoned them, thinking that when they knew we were local it would be all right for her to climb on it when she pleased — but they weren't having it. They made it quite clear that they don't want anybody on the mountain at all."

Hughie frowned. "Shona's never off the mountain in the summer."

"Well, it looks as though this summer's going to be different. I don't want the Americans complaining to Jamie Robertson about us. That's why I came over, Hughie. To warn you to be careful. Taking a wee stag and a salmon now and then, might well land you in hot water."

Hughie looked thoughtful. "Jamie Robertson always knew fine what I was at," he said, looking Ian straight in the eye. "He never minded me taking a salmon for my tea and the only stags I ever shot were auld beasts that would never have lasted the winter — he agreed that it was better for them to be shot cleanly than die, freezing, in a snowdrift."

Ian Ferguson nodded. "I guessed as much," he grinned. "I really came over to sound you out about the Americans. They seem a weird lot. In fact, there's something totally fishy about the whole set-up at the castle. I just can't figure out what it is, though."

"There's always the secret passage that runs from your house to the castle ..." Hughie reminded him.

Ian looked doubtful. "You mean we should spy on them?"

"Well ...?"

"I don't know ... perhaps we should wait for a bit. I mean, they might be perfectly innocent ... and there's Jamie Robertson to consider, too. I'd never be able to look him in the eye again if he ever found out that we'd been spying on his tenants."

Such considerations, however, weren't worrying Shona, for even as her father was discussing the secret passage with Hughie, she was rolling back the fitted carpet in her old playroom. Set flat within one of the flagstones was a heavy round ring.

"Here let me help you," Lewis said as she grasped the ring and hefted the stone upwards. It must have been on some kind of spring for as it rose, it tilted sideways so that it rested against the wall.

"There it is," she said proudly, pointing downwards, "our very own secret passage. It goes all the way to Morven Castle!"

Neil and Clara looked excitedly at the square, black hole that had opened up in the floor.

"How deep is it?" Neil asked, kneeling down to peer into it.

"About six or seven feet," she said shining a torch into its depths, "but Dad put a big, wooden box there so that we can jump down onto it first."

"It smells a bit musty, doesn't it?" Clara said, sniffing the air.

"Mmm. We don't use it all that much. Mostly in the winter when we get snowed in and the drifts are too deep to use the road. Uncle Jamie always invites us for Christmas dinner at the castle and once, when I was small, we took our presents through it with Dad dressed up as Santa Claus. I'll never forget it," she laughed, "it was so exciting!"

"Where does it come out?" Neil asked.

"In the Great Hall of the castle," Lewis said. "Shona took me through it the last time I was here. Of course, she asked Lord Robertson first if we could come and he didn't mind."

"He had tea and cakes ready for us when we reached the hidden door in the panelling and climbed out," Shona grinned. She looked at her watch. "It's a bit late to take you along the passage just now but we could go down tomorrow after dinner. We've got Jennifer to visit in the morning and her mum promised us lunch."

"Sounds like a busy day," Clara smiled.

"Yeah," agreed Neil, his mind still on the secret passage, "and with any luck we might find out what Shane and his lot are up to! I'm just dying to find out!"

It was late when Ian Ferguson left Hughie's cottage and made his way along the dark road towards the shafts of light that streamed from the windows of his house.

Hughie watched him go and sighed. Many years ago, he had made a promise to the Lords of the North that was proving difficult to keep; for while exploring the mountain as a youngster, he had found his way inside.

It was like a dream now, he thought, as he

visualized the blue and silver halls of the Lords of the North. Indeed, if it hadn't been for the little hobgoblins slipping shyly round his door of an afternoon craving biscuits, honey or a piece of cake, he would long ago have decided it was just a childhood fantasy.

Nevertheless, a worried frown creased his forehead as he tidied his kitchen and, like Ian Ferguson, wondered what on earth the Americans were up to in Glenmorven.

13. Jennifer's glen

"Keep going, Lewis," Shona said, pointing upwards. "Once we reach that outcrop of rocks, it's downhill all the way!"

Eventually they reached the top of the ridge and, panting slightly, looked over Glen Garchory; a deep glen that nestled between the steep slopes of high mountains.

"That's Jennifer's house over there," Shona said, pointing towards a white, two-storey building with high gables that was surrounded by a considerable sprawl of barns and outhouses. "Another half an hour and we'll be there."

Lewis was glad to hear it. He wasn't nearly as fit as Neil and Clara and his muscles were already aching.

Jennifer saw them coming and met them half way. She was slim, blonde and wore a heavy sweater over her jeans.

"Hi, Shona! Hi there, Lewis," she said, cheerfully. "Glad you could make it!"

"I warned them that it was a bit of a walk, Jenni," laughed Shona, introducing Neil and Clara.

"You'll be used to it, though," Jennifer said with a laugh. "Lewis tells me you live beside Arthur's Seat! He's the one who needs the exercise!"

"This'll last me for some time, believe me," Lewis groaned. "I'm still stiff from climbing Morven yesterday!"

Mention of Morven reminded Shona of the

Americans. Her temper flared immediately and she looked indignant. "You'll never guess what happened to us yesterday, Jenni," she began and tucking her red hair behind her ears, promptly poured out the whole story of their meeting with Shane and his friends. "And now," she finished, irritably, "I've been banned from climbing Morven." She was still furious at the whole affair and they were so busy discussing it that the last part of the journey passed quickly and in no time at all, they reached the farmhouse.

"Dad's gone into Aberdeen today," Jenni said, opening the front door, "but Mum's making us lunch and after that I thought I might show you round the farm." She looked enquiringly at Neil and Clara.

"Great," Neil smiled.

Her mother put down the telephone as they came into the kitchen. "Anything wrong, Mum?" Jennifer asked, seeing her face.

"Not exactly," Mrs Sinclair smiled at Neil and Clara. She was as blonde as her daughter with bright blue eyes and a wide smile. "Nice to meet you both," she said. "We've heard a lot about you from Lewis. Why don't you sit at the table? Lunch is ready."

"Who were you talking to on the telephone, Mum?" Jennifer persisted, passing round the vegetables as her mother served them with slices of roast chicken. "It's bothering you, isn't it?"

"Not bothering me exactly," her mother said, sitting down and reaching for her napkin. "It was Morag on the phone. You know Morag, don't you

Shona? Well, she was saying that the people in the next glen to her saw a stone giant last night."

"A stone giant?" Jenni looked at her in surprise.

Clara, too, looked up so abruptly that she choked on a mouthful of chicken.

"Here, have a drink of water," Lewis said, pushing the glass into her hand as her face reddened and she coughed.

"You all right, Clara?" Neil managed to keep his voice calm. He had almost choked, too, for in the past they had both come across a stone giant in terrifying circumstances.

"A stone giant? That's impossible," Shona frowned.

"That's exactly what I said," Mary Sinclair nodded as Clara drank some more water and stopped coughing, "but there have been lots of rumours going round of giants appearing on the west coast. I read about them in the paper the other day. Anyway, you know what Morag's like. She'll believe anything."

"Something must have happened for people to talk about a stone giant, though," Jenni pointed out.

"It sounded quite frightening really. Apparently a terrible crash of thunder woke them in the middle of the night and when they looked out of their windows they could see this huge giant walking down the mountainside lit up by the flashes of lightning. They were so scared that they ... well, they left their house and headed for the next glen. Morag said they woke her up in the middle of the night, soaked to the skin and dead scared.

Anyway, they've decided to stay with relatives, near Ballater."

"Did anyone else see the giant?" Neil asked.

"I don't think so. Theirs is a pretty lonely glen," Mrs Sinclair said, "but the next morning, Morag's husband went back with them to look for it and there was absolutely nothing there. Mind you, the storm must have loosened the side of the hill for there was a landslide over the road near the head of the glen. It's quite impassable now," she said.

"So they just imagined the giant, then?" Shona said.

"Well, they certainly didn't find it and if it was as big as they said it was ... well, it would be quite difficult for it to hide."

After lunch, Jenni took them round the farm. Neil pressed Clara's arm and they let the others go ahead into the barn on their own.

"This is turning out to be a very queer holiday, Clara," he said. "Weird Americans, a magic mountain and now — stone giants! What on earth is going on?"

Clara shook her head. "I don't know," she whispered, "but whatever it is, I don't like it. Remember, I *saw* the Old Man of the Mountains," she said as they walked to join the others, "and I'll never forget his face; all rock and stone. He was dead scary!"

Shona and Jenni were crouched over a basket at one end of the barn.

"Oh, aren't they beautiful," Shona was saying to Lewis as they made their way across the barn. "Come and look, Clara; the farm cat has had kittens!"

"Actually, they're old enough to leave their mother, now," Jenni said. "I've found homes for two of them but I'm keeping this one," she showed them a thin, rather ugly-looking tabby and white kitten. "She's really adorable but just so ugly that nobody wants her!" She kissed the kitten and perched it on her shoulder where it clung to her sweater with sharp little claws. I've called her Ugly Mug!" she laughed.

Time flew past as they explored the farm. "Almost three o'clock," Shona remarked as they wandered back to the farmhouse kitchen. "We'll have to think about heading for home, I'm afraid."

"Yes," Jennifer's mother agreed. "You don't want to leave it too late."

As they waved goodbye, Mrs Sinclair glanced round the sweeping slopes of the mountains and shivered slightly as she realized how very lonely the glen was. She'd be glad when her husband returned.

Sharing her mother's thoughts, Jennifer, too, looked warily round the glen and, giving one last wave to Shona and her friends, turned and followed her mother into the house.

"Cheer up, Lewis," Shona grinned as they strode towards the narrow track that led up to the ridge, "once we reach the top, it's downhill all the way!"

"Yes," Clara grinned, "and don't forget that after dinner tonight we're going to go through the secret passage to the castle."

14. The secret passage

"I'm going to show Neil and Clara the secret passage this evening," Shona announced as they were having dinner that evening.

"Haven't you had enough exercise for one day?" her father asked, eyebrows raised.

"Going down a secret passage isn't exercise," Clara smiled. "It's exciting!"

"Well, take a torch each," Mrs Ferguson smiled, "and don't get lost!"

Shona grinned. "We can hardly do that," she said. "It only goes in one direction!"

"And put on an extra sweater," her father warned. "It's quite cold down there."

It was chilly in the secret passage. The cold draught that wafted along made Neil realize that there must be air vents to the surface.

"It's been well made," Lewis said, shining his torch over the old stonework, "a bit damp here and there but not so you'd notice."

"Just mind your head," Shona warned. "It's a bit low in places and mum and dad sometimes have to duck!"

Shining their torches in front of them, the tunnel stretched into the gloom. Although it only took them about a quarter of an hour to reach the castle, it seemed much longer in the dark confines of the secret passage.

"We're here," Shona said, thankfully, as she noticed the change in the stonework. "Not far to go now, so keep your voices down!"

They followed her up a narrow flight of steep, stone steps and soon found themselves in a tall, thin passage. One wall seemed to be made of wood and as she ran her fingers over it, Clara realized that they were walking in a space behind the walls of a room for she could vaguely hear the sound of voices.

Shona stopped and, putting her fingers on her lips, stood on a large stone. The stone had been put there for a reason and, as Clara watched fascinated, Shona balanced herself carefully, slipped back a catch and pushed a tiny piece of panelling to one side. Immediately the voices became clearer and they were very definitely American. Lewis gave Neil the thumbs up sign. They'd done it! Now, with any luck, they might find out just what the Americans were doing in Glenmorven.

"I'm telling you, it's all over Aberdeen," Steve was saying, leaning forward excitedly in his armchair. "People were talking about it in every shop I was in. They're full of it and, I kid you not, they really believe it!"

"What?" Chuck said, frowning slightly. "That there are stone giants in the mountains?"

Shane looked sceptical. "You shouldn't listen to that rubbish. I heard about it on the news and they're playing it down big time. Somebody thinks they see a giant and all of a sudden everybody's seeing giants everywhere!"

"I reckon it might be a good idea to go out and look for them," Sam said, getting to his feet and moving over to a huge wall map of the area. "It's getting kinda boring sitting around here. Whadya say, boys? Fancy a giant hunt?"

"Come off it!" Jake said. "Giants? Look, man, the weather's bad, there's a landslide and maybe it does, for a few seconds, look just like a giant and then — it's gone. And what's left? A pile of rocks and rubble."

"Rocks and rubble," repeated Chuck. "Say ... that's not a bad idea. We talked about it before, remember? Blowing the side off the mountain! These giants are the perfect cover. We just wait for the next thunderstorm and detonate the explosives in the middle of it."

There was a silence. "That," Shane said, "ought to be a piece of cake! We brought explosives with us and you're right ... the next big storm that comes along should give us good cover for an almighty bang."

"Yeah! Nobody would ever guess," Chuck said thoughtfully, "and if anyone did hear the explosion ... well, they'd think it was thunder."

"Or a stone giant, like you said," laughed Sam.

Shona stepped down from her perch on the high stone to give Neil a chance to see into the room. She was seething with rage. Blowing up Morven! How could they even think about it!

Neil, in the meantime was staring in round-eyed wonder through the hole in the panelling. Not, it must be said, at the Americans. Indeed, they were now the least of his worries. He wasn't even listening to them. He was staring, totally and absolutely gobsmacked. No one had mentioned that the castle was haunted yet he could see them quite clearly

— two huge, kilted figures leaning back against an old oak chest. One had a mop of ferocious red hair, the other was dark and sported a black beard and both carried shields and heavy swords. Claymores, he supposed. He was just about to whisper the news to Clara and Lewis when he remembered that Shona knew nothing of their magic past.

"Let's have a look, Neil," Lewis whispered, tugging at his sleeve.

Neil stepped down from the stone, his mind in turmoil. What on earth was going on, he wondered. He tried to catch Clara's eye so that he could warn her about the ghosts. It would be awful if she cried out in surprise and gave the game away! Clara, however, was looking up at Lewis, waiting for her turn to look through the panelling and it was as Neil leant forward to whisper in her ear that Lewis's foot slipped off the stone.

Clara and Shona caught him as he tumbled but it was too late, the damage had been done. They looked at one another in alarm as they heard the Americans push their chairs back at the sudden noise.

"What was that?" Sam said fearfully.

"It came from the wall over there," Chuck said, getting to his feet.

Shona reached up and quickly slid the little piece of panelling back into place as the Americans reached the wall and started tapping it.

"It's hollow," Shane snarled. "There must be somebody behind it!"

"It's probably these wretched ghosts again!"

"Or rats," Steve said, hopefully.

"Quiet, there's someone in there," Shane snapped. "I'm sure I heard something! Listen!"

But, by then, there was nothing to hear for the four children had already reached the steep, narrow stair and were tip-toeing very quietly back along the secret passage.

Clara and Shona looked scared but Lewis was as white as a sheet and it was then that Neil remembered that Lewis, too, was wearing a firestone. That was it! He must have seen the ghosts!

It wasn't only the ghosts that had scared Lewis, however. He'd had another shock, a shock that left his mind reeling, for before he'd slipped off the stone he'd had a good view of Chuck, and he'd recognized him immediately. Chuck, with the funny, spiky haircut, who used to visit his mum and dad in Kuwait. He couldn't believe it. His friend, Chuck, was one of the Americans at Morven Castle!

15. Ambush

Prince Kalman opened his eyes as the noise of a helicopter drowned out the sound of the van's rather decrepit old engine.

Larry peered out of the side window, the bells on his cap rattling against the glass. "There's another helicopter," he said worriedly, "I wonder what it's up to?" They'd noticed a police helicopter hovering above the road as they'd left Crianlarich and he wondered if it was the same one. "It's got its searchlight on," he said, bending his head to get a better look at it as it quartered the mountain slopes. "Do you think they know there are giants around?"

"Bound to," Kenny nodded, glancing at the stag through his rear-view mirror, "I bet the trailer driver stopped at the first police station he came to."

"Most probably," Kalman agreed, remembering the look of horror on the man's face as he'd seen a giant thundering along the road towards him.

"Look out, there's a road block ahead," Larry said as they turned a bend and the headlights lit up the fluorescent jackets of the waiting policemen.

As the van drew closer to the barrier, Kalman became increasingly apprehensive. So far the journey had been long but uneventful as Kenny, who knew the quiet country roads like the back of his hand, had used his knowledge to cut across country. Travelling through the night had been to their advantage as the roads were virtually empty and dawn was still an hour away.

"Can you try and hide the stag, Larry?" Kenny muttered. "The police will ask questions if they see it in the back."

"You nuts or something?" Larry glowered at him in exasperation. "They'll see it whether we cover it up or not. How on earth can I hide a beast that size?"

"They're going to ask us where we got it," panicked Kenny, "and what are we going to say?"

"We'll ... we'll say it's injured and that we're taking it to the vet."

Kenny shot him a withering look. "Gerraway," he said in disgust, "the police will never swallow that!"

"Well, they can't say we poached it," Larry pointed out plaintively, "for the beast's alive and there's not a mark on it! Anyway," he muttered as the van came to a halt, "it's too late now!"

Although the policeman who bent his head to scan the interior of the vehicle raised his eyebrows and blinked at the multi-coloured garb of the occupants, he did not, however, comment on the huge stag that crowded the back of the van. A surprised Kenny gulped and then bit back an expression of surprise as he cast a quick glance in his mirror; for the stag's antlers, that had quite successfully been blocking his view out of the back window ever since Loch Lomond, seemed to have disappeared. He deliberately turned round and scanned the rear of the van as casually as he could and was totally speechless. Apart from their precious guitars and some drums and stuff, the back of the van was empty. The stag had gone, disappeared, vanished.

Gathering his wits together, he concentrated on what the policeman was saying.

"... several rock falls on the road. We've teams out clearing them so just drive slowly and carefully and you ought to be all right."

"Thanks, mate," Larry replied nervously, doing his best to shield the back of the van, "we'll keep our eyes open."

"There's also," and here the police officer looked worried, "there's also been some sightings of these giants that seem to be appearing here and there in the Highlands. Don't go anywhere near them, will you. We don't know how dangerous they are yet."

"We'll steer well clear of them, if we do see them," Kenny assured him as he put the van into gear and, with a friendly wave, drove off.

"I can't believe it," Larry said, "he never so much as mentioned the stag!"

"He didn't mention it 'cos it isn't there," Kenny replied, glancing once again in his mirror. The van swerved violently as he saw that his view was once again obstructed by a spread of antlers.

"Give over," Larry grabbed at the dashboard, "will you look where you're going?"

"But ... but the stag wasn't there when the police stopped us," Kenny stammered. "I looked in the back and it was empty!"

"Well, it isn't empty now," Larry answered, looking back at the stag whose fine head and soft brown eyes regarded him steadily.

"I made myself invisible," Kalman said. "I thought it best."

"Cool," Larry was impressed. "Wow, you really *are* a magician, then!"

"What about those giants the police were on about?" Kenny asked, looking at the stag through the mirror. "It'll be you they're after, like?"

"I'm afraid so," Kalman admitted. "But don't worry. If they spot me, I'll get out and make a run for it. You'll be alright ... they've nothing against you. It's me they're after and they'll stop at nothing to get me."

Kenny looked at the dashboard anxiously. "I'll have to get petrol soon," he muttered. "We're getting low."

"D'you have enough cash?" Larry's question was anxious.

Kenny looked worried. "Maybe we'll find another twenty pound note," he joked.

"Yeah," Larry looked dreamy, for the twenty pound note they'd found in the back of the glove compartment had not only bought them petrol at Crianlarich but they'd managed to treat themselves to a whacking fish supper with loads of chips.

Kalman looked thoughtful. It hadn't taken him long to gather that the Jelly Beans were virtually poverty stricken and managed to scrape by on a very meagre budget. He looked at them with more than a hint of admiration as he found their cheerfulness in the face of dire poverty, quite remarkable. They didn't seem to mind, though, and after only ten minutes' conversation it had become obvious that their music was everything to them. After downing the fish and chips hungrily, they'd taken their guitars out of the van and played him some of their best numbers, their thin faces intent and their feet stamping to the beat. Kalman had tried to look suitably impressed but knew that they weren't all that good; in fact they weren't even passably good. Kenny could only play a few chords on the guitar and Larry's voice was weak. The only reason they carried things off was their obvious enthusiasm and infectious high spirits to say nothing of their ridiculous outfits. It was obvious, too, that the van was their home and the little money they made from what they called "gigs" seemed to go on petrol with very little left over for food. Kalman smiled. He was quite sure that they'd find another twenty pound note in the van — maybe more than one this time.

"There are those police helicopters again," Larry said, bending to look out of the windscreen. "Two of them this time. They've still got their search-lights on. Do you think there are more giants around?"

Kenny, too, leant forward and peered upwards to where the helicopters quartered the mountain-side in long swoops. He put his foot on the brake and clicked the headlights to full beam. If there were giants around then he wanted to have plenty of warning. They travelled in this way for a good few miles before a workman wearing a fluorescent jacket and waving a red flag, stopped them on a bend in the road.

"There's a fall of rock just round the corner,"

the man said looking at them nervously as Kenny
pulled up and rolled the window down. "It was one
o' yon giants," he looked back over his shoulder,
"we saw it collapse."

"Chose a right awkward spot, didn't it," Kenny
remarked. "Good job you're here or I'd have gone
smack into it."

"Give us a few minutes and we'll have it
cleared," the man said. "We're just rolling the
rocks and stuff to the side."

Kenny negotiated the bend carefully but the
workmen had obviously been clearing the road for
some time as, apart from a scatter of small rocks
and clods of earth here and there, he had plenty
of room to get round. It was the next bend that
proved the problem for, as the van swept round
it, a giant was waiting for them. Lunging at the
vehicle, it waved a rocky arm that came crashing
down with mighty force. Kenny swerved desperately so that it missed the roof but dealt the front
mudguard a glancing blow that sent the van spin-
ning and the giant reeling. Fortunately, nothing
was coming in the opposite direction and as Kenny
struggled to right the vehicle, the massive figure
almost lost its balance.

"Put your foot down," Larry screamed as the giant
finally found its feet and started after them. Kenny
didn't need to be told twice and pressed the accelerator to the floor. The road wound in sweeping curves
along the base of the mountain and Kalman, using
magic to see round corners, gave instructions. "Stay
close to the side of the mountain," he said sharply,
"there's a giant on the river side of the road."

Kenny held his breath as the van took the corner at speed and passed an astonished giant who was waiting, arms upraised, to flatten them with the huge boulder it held aloft. This gave them a lead of several minutes for it took the giant some time to turn itself round and give chase.

There was a sudden noise overhead as two helicopters zoomed in on the van to give it cover. "There are two giants," the pilot said into his radio, "massive things, the size of houses. They're chasing a van at the moment. The fellow driving it is going like the clappers, I can tell you!"

The pilot of the second helicopter sounded grim. "We're going to have to stop them, Bill," he said, his eyes following the lumbering figures of the giants. "They're getting too close to that village for comfort. Can you imagine the damage they'll cause if they go on the rampage in the streets?"

"What do you suggest we do? We're not armed!"

"No, but they're not very nifty on their feet, are they? If we buzz them, I reckon we could easily knock them off balance. What do you think?"

"Roger. And we can use the loudspeakers as well! That might confuse them!"

"Right, I'll go in first!"

Kenny and Larry ducked instinctively as the swirling blades of the rotors sounded loud overhead as the first helicopter banked in over the van and headed straight for the giants.

"Would you look at that!" Kenny muttered through dry lips as he watched the attack in his mirrors. "They're attacking the giants!"

"For heaven's sake, keep your foot down,"

pleaded Larry. "This isn't the time to hang around and watch!"

Once again, the van took off at speed and so it was that, jesters hats askew, the petrified Jelly Beans rocketed off and it was only when they'd put a safe distance between the van and the giants that they pulled up at the side of the road and watched, stunned, as the helicopters attacked the massive figures.

The giants ducked as the first helicopter headed straight for them, only lifting clear of their heads at the last moment. The second helicopter then banked in for the attack and using its loudspeakers at full blast, sent waves of shrieking sound round the stone figures. The giants had never known anything like it as, totally disorientated, they stepped aside to avoid the whirling rotors.

The van was now forgotten at the sight of this new threat from the skies. The giants, of course, had no idea what helicopters were but their hatred of dragons was as old as the hills themselves and they had no hesitation in equating the two flying monsters in their minds. "Dragon! Dragon!" the giants growled in their deep, gravelly voices and looked around for rocks to throw at these monsters of the skies.

However, they had no time to bend and pick up rocks. The deafening noise from the loudspeakers confused them and as the helicopters swirled, banked and attacked time after time, the inevitable happened. The giants lost their bearings completely and, in a grinding crash, cannoned into one another.

"Gotcha!" the pilots were ecstatic as they banked and swooped triumphantly over the fallen bodies of the giants.

The first battle had been won.

16. Networking

"You *do* believe me, don't you?" Sir James said, eyeing George Tatler doubtfully.

Tatler looked at him quizzically from under bushy eyebrows. In the course of his work for MI5, he had heard many strange stories in his time but few to rival those told by Sir James which were, by any standards, in a class of their own. "I wouldn't believe everybody who told me a story like that," he agreed, a trifle sardonically, "but then, James, nobody tells faery stories quite like you do. I haven't forgotten last year!"

Sir James relaxed and smiled as he thought of their adventures of the previous year when Prince Kalman had put Scotland under a tartan spell that had left Edinburgh looking like a cross between *Brigadoon* and *Braveheart*. Scotland, then, had really been something else ...

Tatler rose to his feet and moved to stand by the tall windows of Sir James's office. "Actually," he began, "when I first heard of the stone giants, I remembered Clara's story of the Old Man of the Mountains and it crossed my mind that you might be getting in touch with me. So, yes, James, I do believe you. Added to that, I've been getting reports fairly regularly about all the giants appearing in the Highlands."

Sir James joined him at the window and as they both stared speculatively at the steep, green slopes of Arthur's Seat, Tatler shook his head. "Amazing, isn't it, to think that the MacArthurs and Arthur live in there? Sometimes I just can't believe it. Anyway, what are *they* saying about the stone giants?"

"Well, the good news is that they're not supposed to be vicious. All they want to do, according to the MacArthur, is walk about the Highlands in peace."

Tatler raised his eyebrows. "That doesn't tie in with the reports I've been getting, James," he disagreed. "Quite the contrary. The police in the Grampians are out in force. There are lots of giants on the roads up there. Actually, police helicopters were involved in a bit of a battle with the giants yesterday. They're a danger to cars, lorries and buses; anything that moves. Anyway, go on. What else?"

"From the sound of things, he thinks they're still quite weak. If they had all their strength they wouldn't be collapsing all over the place and they'd be much taller than the average house."

"I shouldn't tell you this," Tatler said, looking at him sideways, "but I know for a fact that Whitehall is discussing sending in the army to blast them out of existence."

"Hmmm, well, from what the MacArthur said, I doubt if that'll make much difference. According to him, they could just re-form and rise again as another giant."

Tatler looked thoughtful. "I'll pass that information on!"

"There's another problem, George," Sir James eyed him somewhat anxiously, "maybe it's part

of the same problem as the giants. I'm not quite
sure."

"Can't they solve it by magic?" Tatler asked
hopefully.

"Magic seems to be at the root of it," Sir James
answered. He gestured vaguely. "I seem to learn a
bit more about the MacArthurs each time I meet
them. What I've now discovered is that they rely
on an energy source to keep them alive. It's called
Firestar and it's in a mountain in the Grampians
called Morven."

"An energy source of their own!" Tatler looked
sharply at Sir James and then nodded thoughtfully.
"It makes sense, I suppose. It would explain how
they've managed to live for hundreds of years."

"Well, they've just had the most tremendous
shock. About a month ago, something from our
world locked on to Firestar. I don't quite know
what happened but it almost killed them."

"Locked on?" Tatler queried.

"Apparently, there are hobgoblins in Morven
..." He broke off as Tatler raised his eyebrows and
gave him a peculiar look. "I know, I know," he
said, "the mind boggles, but there *are* hobgoblins
in Morven and they look after the machine that
keeps Firestar running."

"For goodness sake, James, if I'm going to have
to explain all this to the Prime Minister, she'll
have me locked up in the nearest loony bin!"

"No, she won't," Sir James grinned, "not after
what happened last year."

"Nevertheless," Tatler said stiffly, "mentioning
hobgoblins *is* stretching things a bit."

Sir James persevered. "The hobgoblin that was running the machine said that he saw a man on their screen just before the force attacked them."

"Is that possible?"

Sir James shrugged. "Firestar is a magic power, remember. I reckon it must have travelled through the satellite to whoever was monitoring it and picked up his image."

"Satellite," Tatler looked at him sharply.

Sir James nodded. "Or something similar. My guess is that it's probably American. It can hardly be a coincidence that shortly after the attack on Firestar, some Americans rented Morven Castle and its estate."

Tatler raised his eyebrows. "Did they, now."

"It so happens that Bob Grant is stationed in Aberdeen. You remember him? Lewis Grant's father?"

"Ah, yes. Lewis was the Black Shadow, wasn't he?"

Sir James nodded. "Yes, he was the lad that saved all those people from the train wreck on the Forth Road Bridge last year."

"Yes," Tatler nodded, "I'd heard that the family had moved to Aberdeen."

"Actually, Bob's in the States just now, but his office re-routed my call. He was a bit surprised to hear from me, as you can imagine, but when I asked him if he'd heard of any American activity in the area around Aberdeen, he was a bit hesitant."

"Hesitant?"

"Yes ... turns out that a few weeks ago his wife spotted a young chap in Aberdeen that they both knew from their time in the Middle East. A chap called Chuck Easterman. Bob finds it quite surprising that he didn't get in touch. And here's the punchline — he says he's involved with NASA these days."

"Does he, indeed," Tatler said, looking suddenly wary.

"What makes it interesting is that just before I called him, Bob had had a phone call from Lewis, who's on holiday in Glenmorven with Neil and Clara. They're staying with friends and Lewis says that he saw Chuck Easterman in Glenmorven. He's quite sure about it. Chuck used to visit the Grants when Lewis was a kid and apparently he remembers his funny haircut."

"Interesting!"

"It is, for that isn't all he told his father. He told him that now that the Americans have rented the Morven estate, it's out of bounds to everyone in the glen. Apparently Chuck's been going over the mountain since the day he arrived; taking rock samples and using a Geiger counter. They've found nothing, though."

"And how does Lewis know *that*?"

"It was the MacArthur that told me the last bit, actually. They've got ghosts in the castle as spies so he knows everything that's going on."

"*Ghosts,*" Tatler echoed. "Well," he shrugged, after a pause, "after all that's happened, I suppose I shouldn't be too surprised ..."

Sir James grinned. "I've given up being surprised at anything the MacArthurs come up with," he confessed, "but this space business is worrying."

"The satellite theory is interesting," Tatler said musingly. "I wonder if it could be Powerprobe. It's the latest one to go up and it's American."

"What's its mission?"

Tatler paled slightly. "I've heard that it's equipped with specially developed lasers," he admitted. "The Americans are looking for new sources of energy."

"If it locked on to something like Firestar then the reaction must have been massive," Sir James looked at him in horror. "No wonder they sent people in to suss the place out!"

"Without telling us," Tatler pointed out grimly.

"I'd argue that out with them later," Sir James said, brushing diplomatic niceties to one side. "First things first, for if the Americans lock on to Morven again it might mean the end of the MacArthurs. Not only them but Arthur, Lord Rothlan and Lady Ellan, Casimir ... Prince Kalman ... the Sultan ... Amgarad ... and probably a lot of other magicians as well that we've never heard of! We just can't afford to let that happen! You'll have to do something about Powerprobe, George. Right away!"

17. Hughie's cottage

Hughie shut the door against a swirl of driving rain and took their wet coats from them.

"I hope you don't mind," Lewis apologized, "but Neil and I felt we had to come and see you on our own. Clara and Shona are helping Mrs Ferguson in the kitchen so we slipped off without them knowing."

Both boys moved over to the fireplace, holding their hands out to the warm blaze of logs in Hughie's kitchen.

"We couldn't tell Shona we were coming," Lewis confessed, "because she doesn't wear a firestone and she doesn't know that you're ... well ... magic, like us."

"So you felt that, did you?" Hughie looked at them shrewdly. "I sensed it in you, too," he admitted, "and I asked Prince Casimir about you. He told me that you wore firestones and knew Lord Rothlan and Prince Kalman."

"Prince Casimir?" Lewis looked thunderstruck. "He's here?"

"Well, he's in Morven," Hughie answered.

"But ... why would he be in Morven?" Lewis looked puzzled.

"Does Morven have magic people inside it, like Arthur's Seat?" guessed Neil.

"Well, there are the hobgoblins, I suppose ..."

"Hobgoblins?" Neil repeated, startled, as he remembered the little creatures they had seen on Morven.

"Do they have faces like goats and slanted yellow eyes?" interrupted Lewis.

Hughie nodded. "Nice little things," he said with a smile. "The Lords of the North call them the Rumblegrumbles."

"So *that's* what we saw when we were on Morven," Lewis said, looking at Neil as another piece of the mystery fell into place, "hobgoblins!"

"What have the Lords of the North got to do with them?" Neil asked curiously.

"Well, they live together in the mountain. Didn't you know?"

Neil and Lewis looked at one another. "We knew Morven was a magic mountain," Neil said slowly, "but we didn't know it was the home of the Lords of the North."

"Then," Hughie said, seriously, "you won't have heard of the attack on Firestar?"

"Firestar?" Lewis looked puzzled. "What's Firestar?"

Hughie told them and both boys looked horrified as he filled them in on what had happened in the mountain.

"Are the Americans involved?" Neil asked. "Is *that* why they're here?"

"Shona took us along the secret passage and we heard them talking," Lewis admitted, looking slightly shamefaced. "We've been trying to find out what they were up to on the mountain."

"And I saw ghosts," Neil added. "Two of them. They looked quite ... er, fearsome."

"The Americans were talking about the giants,"

Lewis continued. "They wanted to use them as an excuse to blow up Morven."

"Shona," Neil said with a grin, "was furious."

"Aye, she would be," Hughie answered, "but you don't need to worry about that," he smiled. "It'll never happen. The ghosts you saw — Red Rory MacGregor and the Black MacTavish — they passed the news on to Prince Casimir. So if, by any chance, the Americans *do* try to blow up the mountain, they'll find that their explosives won't work. The hobgoblins told me that Prince Casimir's hexed them already."

"Cool," Lewis said, grinning at the thought of the useless explosives.

"But what was it that attacked Firestar?" Neil asked.

Hughie frowned. "It seems to have been an American satellite that did the damage," he observed, "but from what the ghosts say, they don't think the Americans know that what they did harmed anybody. They want to get into Morven to find out what's inside it. They never will, of course. The Lords of the North put a protective shield round it that they'll never be able to break ... unless ..."

"Unless there's another attack on Firestar," finished Lewis.

Hughie nodded. "And there will be," he said gravely. "Quite soon, too. The ghosts say that the Americans are waiting for their satellite to lock on to Morven again and the Lords of the North aren't sure if Firestar will be able to withstand another attack. It's quite an anxious time for them."

At that moment, there was a tap on Hughie's kitchen door. Lewis and Neil looked up as it was pushed open and two little hobgoblins trotted confidently over the tiled floor towards the fire. Then they saw Hughie's visitors and froze, their tendrils curling out from their heads.

"It's all right, Rumbletumble," Hughie smiled. "Lewis and Neil are wearing firestones and they can see you."

The hobgoblins tendrils positively shot out of their heads at this alarming news and it was only when Hughie rose to his feet and took their hands in his that they trotted forward and bowed gravely, still looking apprehensive.

"You've arrived just in time to have some tea and cakes with us," Hughie smiled, laying a couple of cushions on either side of the fire. This was obviously their favourite spot and as they plumped themselves down and warmed their little hands, they looked at him expectantly, smiling with funny, toothy grins that made Neil hide a smile.

"We saw you on Morven, didn't we?" Lewis said gently for the hobgoblins looked so nervous that he thought they might take to their heels and run if he spoke any louder. Their attention, however, was fixed on Hughie as he brought over a plate of tiny cakes and laid it between them. Their eyes positively shone and, oblivious to everyone else, they started to eat the cakes, taking little, delicate bites to make each one last longer.

Hughie regarded them with an indulgent smile, knowing that until they finished, conversation was impossible.

"Well, now," Hughie asked, once they'd worked their way through half the plate, "what's the gossip from the hill?"

"There's just been the most awful row at the castle," Rumbletumble said, gleefully.

Hughie raised his eyebrows. "What about?" he asked, interestedly.

"Shane wants to go on a giant hunt," Rumbletumble said excitedly.

"They want to go into the glens to find the giants and see what they're made of," added Rumbletummy, words spilling out of him. "They're all mad keen on the idea — except Chuck, that is. He thinks it's too dangerous!"

"And," Rumbletumble added excitedly, "they've just this minute left the castle. It's true, Hughie," he assured him. "Red Rory MacGregor and the Black MacTavish have just finished telling Prince Casimir so we came down to pass on the news. They say that Chuck's as mad as fire!"

Lewis looked at Neil at the mention of Casimir's name and fingered the magic ring that Casimir had given him in Edinburgh. It'd be great to see him again ...

"I think the scientists have been a bit bored," Rumbletumble explained. "They're more or less just hanging around waiting for their satellite to come back again."

"They're really excited about the giants, though," Rumbletummy pointed out. "They didn't believe in them at first, but now that they're in all the newspapers ... well, they're determined to go out looking for them. You should see the Great Hall.

The dining table is covered with maps and they've been glued to the radio all day. Shane's worked out that the giants will appear in Glen Crannach next."

Neil and Lewis looked at one another in horror for Glen Crannach was very near Jennifer's glen.

"I don't think I'd like to go out on a night like this with giants around," Neil shivered. "It's pouring with rain and the thunder's dreadful."

Hughie frowned. "It's stone-giant weather! Just the kind they like!"

18. Old friends meet

Lewis listened absent-mindedly to Neil's excited remarks as they walked back along the country road that led to Glenmorven House, turning over everything Hughie had said in his mind. Chuck was in the castle ... Chuck was involved in all this ... but why?

"What gives, Lewis?" Neil sounded exasperated. "I don't think you've heard a word I've said."

"Sorry," Lewis admitted, coming to a quick decision. "I've been thinking and ... well, there's something I have to tell you, Neil."

Neil looked at him in surprise. "Shoot," he said, wondering what it was that had brought such a serious look to Lewis's face.

"Remember when I fell off the stone in the secret tunnel?"

"Yeah ... I nearly fell off it as well when I saw the ghosts," Neil grinned.

"It wasn't the ghosts that gave me the fright — although they were scary enough."

Neil looked at him. "What was it then?"

"I recognized one of the Americans," Lewis admitted. "The one with the spiky haircut."

"I saw him," Neil answered. "He looked ... well ... a bit out of place, somehow ..."

"Don't let the haircut fool you," Lewis said seriously. "According to my dad, he's got an absolutely brilliant brain. His name's Chuck and my mum and dad knew him when he was in the Middle

East. His company was building an Earth Satellite Station or some such thing."

"That would fit in with what Hughie was talking about."

"I just can't believe he's involved in all this," Lewis muttered, shaking his head. "I hero-worshipped him! I was a kid at the time but he wasn't too grand to get down on his hands and knees and help me with my Meccano set."

"So?" Neil queried.

"Well, according to the ghosts," Lewis pointed out, "Chuck is on his own in the castle just now. The others have all gone out hunting giants ... so, I was thinking that it might be ..."

"... a good time to pay a visit?" Neil finished the sentence for him.

"Yeah! What do you think? How about it?"

Neil frowned. "Shona said that they keep the castle gates closed."

"Yes, but I don't think they'll be locked. There's no one around here that would pinch anything and to actually lock the gates would cause comment. I mean, people would wonder what they had to hide."

As it happened, the gates weren't locked and as the two boys slipped through warily, they fervently hoped that Shane and the others had already left the castle grounds. Lewis, certainly, didn't fancy meeting them in such a lonely spot for the curving driveway was a secretive, gloomy place. Aware that they were on someone else's land they kept guiltily to the trees at side of the road where banks of snowdrops and daffodils sagged limply in the rain.

It was only when they scrunched across the gravel to the massive main entrance that Neil wondered how they were going to attract attention.

"There doesn't seem to be a bell," he whispered.

"I'll knock," Lewis said, thumping loudly on the heavy door. Nothing happened and they were just about to repeat the process when the door opened and Chuck stood there in a heavy sweater and a pair of disreputable jeans.

"Chuck!" Lewis beamed delightedly. It was as though all the pleasant memories of childhood had returned in a single swoop. He forgot about the satellite, Morven and Firestar in his delight at seeing an old friend.

His pleasure was totally disarming and no one, least of all Chuck, could doubt that it was real.

Chuck stared at him and then recognition dawned. "It's Lewis, isn't it," he grinned. "Well, well, who would have thought it — after all this time! You've grown a bit since I last saw you."

"This is my friend, Neil MacLean," Chuck introduced him. Neil shook Chuck's hand and saw puzzlement flare in his eyes. *He's wondering how we knew he was here,* Neil thought and wished that they had talked things through before embarking on this somewhat dangerous escapade.

"Come in," Chuck ushered them inside. He really had to, thought Lewis. He couldn't keep them standing outside in the cold without seeming rude.

The hall of the castle was pleasantly warm and they headed automatically for the fireplace where a huge fire blazed up the chimney.

"I know it's a bit early in the day to light a fire," Chuck said, "but castles aren't famous for their central heating."

The two boys smiled politely but their faces changed as they saw the ghosts. Chuck noticed and wondered what was wrong. As far as he could see, their eyes seemed focused on a display of swords, cutlasses, claymores and other weapons of war that decorated one of the walls, but why they should exchange worried glances was beyond him.

It so happened that both Lewis and Neil had forgotten all about the ghosts and the knowledge that every word of their conversation would be sent back to the Lords of the North, wasn't lost on them.

"Have a cola?" Chuck offered, producing two cans and a couple of glasses. "Sorry, things are a bit basic here."

They accepted the drinks and for a few moments there was an awkward silence broken only by the gurgle of cola splashing into their glasses, the gentle hiss of flames and the odd crackle from the burning logs.

After asking about Lewis's parents and hearing about his new school in Aberdeen, Chuck came straight to the point. "What puzzles me, Lewis, is how you knew I was here at all," he said, his brown eyes alert. "I haven't been around a lot since we got here and I haven't met the Fergusons, the family you're staying with ..."

Lewis looked embarrassed and, to Neil's amazement, came out with the truth. "We were exploring a secret passage that runs from

Glenmorven House to the castle, here," he said innocently enough. "We were really annoyed the other day because your friends chucked us off Morven and well ... we wanted to know why."

Chuck raised his eyebrows. A secret passage, he thought. Well, it certainly explained the strange noises behind the panelling. Mentally, he scanned his memory, trying to remember what they'd all been talking about at the time.

"You were talking about the giants and blowing up the mountain to get inside it," Lewis answered the question for him and shooting him a straight glance, asked sharply. "Why are you here, Chuck? Is it anything to do with a satellite?"

Chuck was so surprised that from lounging back comfortably in his chair, he sat up straight. "Satellite?" he queried, his face heavy with suspicion. "What do you know about satellites?"

"I thought that's what you did?" Lewis pretended to be puzzled. "It's what you were doing in Kuwait, wasn't it? I was only young at the time but I remember mum and dad talking about it."

Chuck relaxed but his eyes were watchful. "I suppose a satellite does come into the picture, but actually at the moment I'm heading a team of geologists. That's why they've been going over the mountain. They're looking for mineral deposits. There's no secret about it," he said casually, "but I'd rather you didn't mention it to anyone. I mean, Lord Robertson knows about it but I'd really rather keep our work quiet in case we *do* come across anything. I hope you'll bear that in mind," he said pointedly to Lewis. "You can tell your mum and dad, of course. I know they'd keep it to themselves."

"Oh, I've told them already," Lewis looked surprised. "Dad phoned me from the States the other day and I told them you were here, living in a castle."

Chuck's expression didn't change but a shade of annoyance flickered in his eyes. He knew Bob Grant of old; an astute operator with lots of contacts. If he found out about his involvement with Powerprobe then he'd most certainly wonder why he was suddenly holed up in a castle in the wilds of Scotland.

"This is a fabulous place to live," Neil said, looking round, seemingly uninterested in the conversation. "Could I have a look at all these swords and things on the wall?"

"Sure," Chuck got to his feet and they wandered over to the fan-shaped display of weapons. Now thoroughly suspicious, he wondered if Neil had suggested the move to get closer to his computer. Print-outs littered his desk and although they were meaningless to someone his age, they didn't really look like anything vaguely connected to geology.

Lewis, who had been trained at an early age that it was the height of bad manners to try to read anything on anybody's desk, was actually wondering much the same thing but, as it turned out, Neil was genuinely interested in the weapons.

"I'd take one down to show you," Chuck said, glad that the conversation had taken a new direction, "but they're more or less anchored to the wall. When we first arrived, we wanted to see how heavy the swords were but we couldn't shift them — short of digging the stanchions out of the wall, that is.

"We read a poem called *The Charge of the Light Brigade* last term," Neil admitted shyly, "and there was a fantastic picture of it in the book — the horsemen charging the guns with only swords in their hands."

"I know the one you mean," Chuck said, his expression changing. "Most people tend to think of it as a dreadful waste of life but the Light Brigade overran the Russian guns, you know, and changed the course of the war."

"It must be hard to be really brave," Lewis said thoughtfully.

Chuck looked at him oddly. "Oh, I think both of you would measure up," he said with a grin.

Lewis saw the smile and taking advantage of it asked tentatively. "Since you know us, Chuck, do you think we could go on the mountain from time to time? I mean, Shona, the Ferguson's daughter, really loves Morven and ..." Lewis tailed off looking at Chuck hopefully.

So that, thought Chuck with some relief, is why they really came. He softened the blow as much as he could. "I'm sorry, Lewis," he said, grinning at him ruefully, but sounding serious at the same time, "really sorry, but I'm afraid I can't give anyone permission to go on the mountain."

The two ghosts, in all their tartan finery, had been following the conversation for some time but at his words, their expressions changed swiftly from the mildly interested to the totally ferocious.

They were, in their own way, very fond of Shona and, as Neil and Lewis watched, they exchanged determined nods before stepping up to Chuck and hugging him fiercely.

Chuck drew in a gasping breath as he shivered convulsively in the blast of cold air that froze him to the marrow but not before he noticed that the two boys were looking, not at him, but at something or someone behind him.

19. Hunting giants

Despite the poor visibility and totally foul weather, Shane and his little group of geologists moved steadily across the glens and passes of the mountains. Young, fit and unhindered by the heavy packs they usually carried, they covered the ground in long easy strides, taking care to give isolated houses and crofts a wide berth.

"This should be it," Shane said as they finally topped the summit of a ridge. "Glen Crannach"

A jagged streak of lightning lit the length and breadth of the glen that stretched before them. A road ran along the foot of the mountains and telephone poles spoke of civilization somewhere but the darkness was unbroken by lights of any sort.

"I can't see any houses," Sam said, viewing the isolation with disfavour.

"I can't see any giants, either, Sammy," announced Jake, sourly. Of all of them, he had been the least enthusiastic. As far as he was concerned, ghosts and stone giants were the figments of particularly vivid imaginations and he was having none of it.

Shane ignored him and, making their way downhill, they crouched in the lee of a massive stone cliff where they were protected to a certain extent from the worst of the driving rain. Huddling under waterproof hoods, they settled down to wait for the stone giants to arrive.

It was Steve who felt the ground stir beneath

him. "Hey, the ground's moving!" he said in alarm as the slope beneath him heaved gently.

Shane felt it, too. "Maybe the rain's loosened the hillside," he snapped. With one accord they looked up at the towering cliff that loomed above them.

It was then that they saw that the cliff seemed to be leaning towards them.

"Come on, let's get out of here!"

They were brave men, all of them, but they turned white with horror. The cliff was immense and they knew they were going to have to move swiftly if they were going to survive.

"Run!" snapped Shane and, reacting instinctively to the command, they scrambled for safety.

Panting with fear, more than exertion, they managed to reach a rocky bluff and, clinging on grimly, stopped to look back. Expecting to see the cliff collapse into the valley below, they were stunned to see a very different sight; for the cliff did not fall but had become the massive head and shoulders of a giant figure that was heaving and tearing itself from the slopes of the mountain.

Terrified, they watched as huge rocks and stones fell from it and bounced into the depths of the glen. Great legs, pillars of rock, flexed at the knees and arms flailed wildly as the giant rose from the mountain and became mobile. Lightning flashed in vicious, jagged streaks as with a great roaring noise, it started to walk and they backed away in horror as they realized that it was walking towards them.

"Scatter, and make for higher ground," Shane yelled as he saw the giant's massive, rocky feet crushing the ground as it moved in huge strides towards them.

"There are more giants on the other side of the valley! I can see at least two," Steve called.

"Let's get out of here," Shane yelled back.

They ran frantically for the head of the glen but the giants seemed able to see them and followed them towards the ridge.

Then Sammy tripped and fell. Shane heard Jake scream. "Sammy's down!"

With one accord they turned and saw Sammy lying helplessly in the path of the giant's feet. Shane saw the monstrous face of the giant change and knew that it had seen Sammy. Sick with fear, he ran forward, shouting "No! No!"

It was useless, he knew. Nothing could stop the huge figure that towered above him and, screaming at it, he watched in amazement as, although the great head had no eyes that he could see, the giant seemed to notice him. It stopped and then, very deliberately, changed its course and walked around Sammy.

Sammy then rolled down a slope to safety and Shane found that in trying to save him, he himself, was now in the path of the monstrous figure. So terrified was he that he froze in his tracks and watched as the great legs crushed the mountainside — and again changed direction! The giant, it seemed, had deliberately left its path to walk around him. The other two giants made no attempt to approach them at all but plodded ponderously on, their sighted, but eyeless, faces fixed firmly on the head of the glen.

Shane took a deep breath and ran to where Sammy lay crouched in the lashing rain, shaking with terror. "It had no eyes," he said, "but it looked at me and didn't step on me. It could have done," he gabbled, "but it didn't."

"Yeah, yeah, I know. Come on, Sammy. Let's get you out of here. Can you walk?"

"Sure I can walk," Sammy said. "No bones broken either."

"Right. Let's stay together and get out of here. The giants are ahead of us now."

"Look, there they are," Jake pointed dramatically at the ridge where the three huge giants stood, outlined dramatically against the skyline.

"If we cut off to the right, we might be able to see where they're going," Shane said. "Come on, let's go!"

As the thunder rolled and lightning streaked the sky, they covered the ground as quickly as possible and reached the next glen, hoping that they had managed to overtake the huge creatures.

"Where are they?" Jake asked as he turned to see how far the stone giants had reached.

"I can't see them at all," Sammy said, blank amazement in his voice. A sudden flash of lightning lit the glen and, in the few seconds of brightness, they saw that it was empty. There were no stone figures to be seen.

"They've disappeared!"

"They can't have!"

"Come on, they must be somewhere!"

"But where did they go? There's nowhere here for them to hide and they were huge. Much bigger than a house."

"Look there," Sammy pointed. "Those rock falls weren't there before, were they?"

"No," Shane agreed. "No, you're right, they weren't."

They looked at one another in silence.

"Do you think the giants have gone back to being part of the mountain again?" Steve conjectured, surveying the fallen remains doubtfully.

Sammy looked at the tumble of rocks and earth. "I think they have," he said, bending down and picking up a piece of black rock. "I think that's what's been happening all over Scotland. They grow and they die."

"I've never believed in magic," Jake said as he, too, bent and picked out a rock from the landslide, "but I do now. They were fantastic! Out of this world! I'm going to keep this as a souvenir."

"Good idea," nodded Shane as they all bent and chose pieces of rock. "I'll never forget tonight," he said. "Strange, isn't it, that the giants avoided stepping on us. It shows that they are intelligent. It could easily have crushed me, but it didn't."

Steve nodded. "At first, I thought they were chasing us, but they weren't, really, you know," he said, turning his piece of rock over in his hand and looking at it thoughtfully. "They were going somewhere definite and it just so happened that we stood in their way."

"But they didn't get far, did they?"

"No, I can't think why, either. They were certainly powerful enough. Maybe ... well, maybe their magic just ran out on them."

"But where were they going?" Shane wondered slowly. "And why?"

Although they hadn't noticed it, the weather had started to clear and in the fitful moonlight they could see far over the mountains. Steve flung out his hand and pointed. "*I* reckon they were going *there*," he said.

They were suddenly still, silent and alert for, rising in the distance, sharp and clear, dominating the landscape, was the tall, hump backed shape of a very familiar mountain.

Steve's voice was grim as he turned towards them. "*I* reckon they were heading for Morven!" he said.

20. Stag at bay

"Would you *just* look at them!" Kenny gasped, pulling up in a lay-by that gave them a glimpse of the road ahead, for about half a mile further on, a group of at least six giants barred their way.

Kalman's heart sank as he peered at the wall of giants that stood threateningly across the road.

Larry turned white. "Oh boy!" he muttered, his face the colour of chalk, "they're really out to get us, aren't they!"

Inside the van, fear now replaced the atmosphere of easy friendship that had grown between the Jelly Beans and the stag.

"It's too dangerous for me to stay with you any longer," Kalman observed. "Don't worry, I'll get out here and take to the hills." He flung the giants an assessing glance, knowing that the van wouldn't stand a chance if they were to attack it. "It'll be all right," he assured them, "when they see me on the hill, they'll leave you alone." He looked at them grimly. "I'd hoped that we might get closer to Ballater before they stopped us but at least I'm rested now."

"But Ballater's miles away," Larry protested. "The giants might still catch you!"

"Hang on! Don't get out here," Kenny said, swiftly reversing the van and driving back the way they'd come. "We passed a lay-by a while back that gives onto the mountain," he explained, "and further up I noticed a pass. If you cross it, I reckon you might save a bit of time, for the road takes the long way round. Show him the map, Larry."

Larry fished in the glove compartment and drew out a rather tattered ordnance survey map. Folding it to where they were on the road, he pointed to the pass and a way across the mountains that would, indeed, cut a huge chunk from the stag's journey.

Kenny drew up when they reached the bottom of the grassy slope that rose towards the break in the mountains. "That's the way to go," he said, nodding towards the pass. He switched off the engine and clambered out to open up the back of the van for the stag. Kalman backed his way down onto the road, feeling the stag's hooves scrabble to get a grip on the tarmac. His antlers proved more of a problem but by carefully turning his head Kenny finally extricated the increasingly panic-stricken stag.

Once clear of the van, the stag lifted its head and stretched its legs with a sigh of relief. The mountain air was fresh and clean and it was glad to be free of the confined space inside the dreadful machine. Concentrating his mind, Kalman calmed the stag and brought it under his control again. Seeing the anxious faces of Larry and Kenny, he felt a twinge of remorse at having put them in such a position and knowing that their danger was real, he stepped forward, gently resting the stag's head on their shoulders. They thought it was his way of saying thank you for their help but it was more than that, for he was using more of his precious magic to give them what protection he could.

"Thank you," Kalman said, "you'll never know

how grateful I am to you. But you'd better hurry for the giants are on their way already."

Despite the approach of the giants, Larry and Kenny watched in fascinated wonder as the great stag leapt swiftly onto the rough grass and heather of the mountainside and headed up the steep incline towards the pass that would take it deeper into the mountains and closer to Morven. Larry's eyes clouded with unaccustomed tears as he clambered into the van and watched it through the windscreen. "I'll never forget that stag, Kenny," he said as he watched it bound upwards, "it was a miracle, like."

"What we're needing is another one then," Kenny snapped, pulling out of the lay-by and looking worriedly in the rear-view mirror. "Here come the giants!"

He'd left it a bit late for, even as he took off along the narrow road that hugged the side of the mountain, the giants closed in on the van, roaring and shouting in strange gravelly voices that raised the hair on the back of their necks.

Kalman, however, had made a gross miscalculation in assuming that the giants would see him on the mountainside. They only had eyes for the van and it soon became apparent to Kenny and Larry that the giants didn't know that the stag was no longer there. Totally petrified, Kenny put his foot to the floor and the engine screamed in protest as they rocked and bucketed their way round the many hairpin bends in the road. It was then that a press helicopter soared into view and, as the cameras rolled, horrified viewers all over Scotland saw the giants charging after the speeding vehicle.

"Use the loudspeaker to warn them," shouted the pilot suddenly to the TV crew for he could see more giants rising from the mountains ahead of the van. It was well and truly trapped. Kenny, with a face as white as chalk, stepped on the brakes as he saw the huge figures appear in front of him and Larry grabbed his arm in terror as the giants closed in on them. Controlled by Lord Jezail, the giants had their instructions. The van had to be destroyed ... and that was what they did.

The giants didn't try to push the car off the road or deliberately thump it with their great hands — they gathered together in a roaring crowd round the van and collapsed on top of it, burying Kenny and Larry under a massive heap of rocks, stones and rubble.

The crew in the helicopter filmed the entire thing, the machine hovering helplessly as clouds of dust filled the air. Alerted by the TV crew, however, rescue services were already on their way and by the time the fire engines, police cars and ambulances arrived, the dust had settled. Apart from the clatter of the helicopter's rotors, everything was quiet. The giants had finished their work.

No one held out much hope for Kenny and Larry. "It'll be a miracle if they're alive under that lot," one of the TV crew said, as the helicopter swooped and banked, unable to get as close as they would have liked to the side of the mountain. "They didn't stand a chance. Their van must have been flattened."

It took some time for the team of men to remove

the rocks, passing them from hand to hand until the van's bright fluorescent paintwork emerged. There was a sudden cheer as the men worked with renewed energy to clear the remaining boulders and gasps of amazement from those in the helicopter as the van doors were prised open and Kenny and Larry staggered out into the road.

"It's incredible," the newscaster said, his voice shrill with relief. "They both seem to be fine. I can see them walking and talking to the firemen. They're waving to us! *What* an ordeal!"

Kenny and Larry were treated for shock at the local hospital. Outside, reporters and television crews were kept firmly out of the way until the following morning when they'd agreed to give a press conference. Offers for their story, however, were already flooding in.

"One paper's offering us fifty thousand pounds to tell them what happened," Larry said, totally gobsmacked. "Just think, Kenny," his eyes were alight with excitement, "with that amount we could really make something of the band! Maybe hit the big time even!"

"It's a miracle that you survived at all, you know," one of the nurses told them as they got ready to leave the next morning. "The firemen can't understand how the rocks didn't flatten your van completely. You can thank your lucky stars that you came through it all without a scratch!"

"It was the stag's magic that saved us, wasn't it," Larry whispered as the nurse waved them goodbye and they set off along the passage towards a waiting policeman. "I'm sure of it."

Kenny nodded. "We'd better no' mention the stag to these reporters, though," he cautioned, thinking of the forthcoming press conference, "for there's no way they'd publish our story if we start talking about magic. They'd just think we were basket cases."

"Aye," Larry agreed, "best to stick to us being the Jelly Beans and looking for gigs in Aberdeen."

"Up with the Jelly Beans!!" grinned Kenny, suddenly triumphant. "Larry, mate," he grabbed him by the shoulders and looked into his eyes, "Larry, mate! I think our luck is finally changing!"

21. Night flight

"Ian," Helen Ferguson sat up in bed, "Ian, wake up!" She eyed the alarm clock in disbelief as she shook her husband again. "Ian, wake up! Somebody's knocking at the door! It's three o'clock in the morning!"

"Dad," Shona ran into the bedroom in her pyjamas, "Dad! Get up! There's somebody at the door!"

Ian Ferguson woke from a deep sleep and looked at Shona blankly as she tugged at the duvet. "Quick, Dad! See who it is!"

Mrs Ferguson tied the cords of her dressing-gown and slipped her feet into a pair of slippers.

"What's going on?" her husband muttered. "What time is it?"

"Three o'clock."

"Three o'clock! In the morning!" He put his feet in his slippers. "Who on earth can it be," he muttered, heading for the stairs.

By this time Neil, Clara and Lewis were awake, too, and peering round their bedroom doors, watched in alarm as Shona's dad went downstairs.

"Ian, Ian," a voice shouted urgently, "it's Peter Sinclair! Can you open the door? We're freezing!"

Ian unlocked the door and pulled back the chain. The blast of cold air that swept in made them all shiver as Peter Sinclair, his wife and Jennifer all tumbled hurriedly into the hall.

Ian shut the door hastily against the icy draught. "Peter," he said, looking at him in disbelief; for under their overcoats the Sinclairs were still in their nightclothes. Helen Ferguson took one look at the shivering group and turned the thermostat up to full.

Jennifer *was* frozen. The journey over the mountains had been a nightmare and she had made it with only a coat over her nightie and bare legs thrust into a pair of trainers. Shona, knowing only too well the distance they had travelled, looked at her worriedly. Jennifer was not only cold, she was trembling with fright. "We saw them," she whispered to Shona. "We saw the giants! They were in our glen!"

There was no more sleep for anyone that night. The storm outside shrieked and whistled as, clutching mugs of coffee and hot chocolate they huddled round the embers of the living room fire. Ian stirred them into life and deftly adding more logs, nursed the flames until a blazing fire roared up the chimney.

For a few minutes, the Sinclairs just stared into the fire, still shocked from their ordeal.

"What happened, then, Peter?" Ian asked tentatively.

"It was in my mind that they'd soon be reaching our glen." Peter said, sipping his coffee gratefully. "I kept watch from our bedroom window but I couldn't see much for the storm. It was the most amazing thing, Ian. There was a lot of lightning and I saw them, then. They just seemed to rise from the slopes of the mountainside. I woke Mary and we got Jennifer out of bed, flung on our coats and took off into the night. They were close behind us and moving at quite a speed. We could hear the crash of their footsteps!"

"They? You mean there was more than one?"

"I saw three of them."

Ian half-started from his chair. "Where are they now?" he asked in alarm. "Did they reach our glen?"

Mary Sinclair shook her head. "One of them reached the top of the ridge," she said, "we saw it quite clearly against the skyline — and then," she hesitated, "it was quite sad really. It seemed to grow bigger for a few seconds and then it just crumbled away."

Her husband nodded. "The old stories of the Cri'achan are coming true, Ian. They're walking the hills." He held out his hands to the fire and paused. "That's why I've decided to move out," he admitted. "I'm taking Mary and Jennifer to Aberdeen when it gets light. I was wondering ... do you think Hughie will lend us his car?"

"Don't be silly, Peter," Ian said immediately. "I'll drive you there myself. Going to stay with your mother, are you?"

"Yes, until this all blows over," was the answer.

"If the giants get any closer," Ian said thoughtfully, "then we'll be moving out, as well."

"Leave Glenmorven!" Shona sat up, her face a picture of horror. "Dad, what are you saying? We can't leave the glen!"

Neil, Clara and Lewis looked at one another.

"I think you children should go back to bed,

now, for what's left of the night," Shona's mother fussed, suddenly worried that too much was being said in front of her guests. "Jenni looks exhausted, poor thing. Let her share your bed tonight, Shona," she added. "She's been through a lot."

Jennifer did look white and strained. "Come on, Jenni," Lewis said as they all got to their feet. "It's over now."

"And just think of the tales you'll have to tell when we get back to school," Shona added, trying to coax a smile out of her. "It's not everyone that's seen a stone giant!"

Jenni grinned weakly but it was only when she reached the bedroom that she started to cry. "It's Ugly Mug," she wept, sitting on the edge of Shona's bed, twisting a tissue in her hands. "Dad wouldn't let me look for her. He said there was no time but it would only have taken me a minute to grab her."

"Surely her mother will feed her," Clara pointed out.

Jennifer shook her head. "Mitzi's in Aberdeen at the vet. And if Ugly Mug's left alone, she'll starve!"

Shona looked at Clara and nodded understandingly. Ugly Mug meant everything to Jenni. The kitten was her friend and playmate.

"Don't cry, Jenni," Shona said, putting an arm round her. "The stone giants have gone. You heard what your mother said. They broke up, didn't they?" She glanced at Clara. "So there's no reason why we shouldn't go back to your house tomorrow to get Ugly Mug."

Clara nodded. "We'll take some cat food with us so that we can catch her."

"And," added Shona, "if *we* end up in Aberdeen with my gran, we'll be able to give her back to you, how's that?"

"We'll be okay. We'll all go," Clara said, seeing Jenni's worried face. "It won't take that long, will it?" She looked at Shona for back-up.

Shona grinned. "If we hurry, it'll only take us a couple of hours at the most to get there and back."

Jennifer's face lit up as she scrubbed the tears from her face with a tissue that was already sodden.

Clara smiled. "We'll all go together," she said, "and we'll bring Ugly Mug back with us!"

22. Lord Rothlan

Seated on silver thrones in the halls of the Lords of the North, Prince Casimir talked anxiously to Lord Rothlan and his wife, Lady Ellan, who had just arrived from their castle at Jarishan. There had been a wonderful display of fireworks over the mountain to greet them and now that they had paid their respects to the old Lords, they were anxious to get up to date with what was happening. Amgarad, Rothlan's great eagle, perched on his shoulder and listened attentively to what was being said for never before had there been such a crisis in the world of magic.

"And the stone giants?" queried Rothlan later, when they'd finished discussing Firestar. "What's brought *them* to life?"

Casimir shook his head. "I just don't know, Alasdair," he said frankly. "This attack has upset everything. Nothing is as it was before — and now that the Cri'achan are awake and walking the mountains, it makes one wonder what else might have risen from the depths of the earth."

Amgarad, perched on the arm of Rothlan's chair, hunched his back and made an indescribable noise. Rothlan dropped his eyes. "Not a pleasant thought," he murmured.

"Exactly," Casimir agreed, "and as for the Cri'achan … well, they seem to have changed, and not for the better."

"Changed?" Lady Ellan looked at him enquiringly.

Casimir nodded. "They used to be quite peace-able in the old days but since they've risen, they seem to have become aggressive and they're head-ing eastwards, you know — quite definitely in this direction. Firestar's power must be drawing them."

"I'm surprised that Lord Alarid hasn't done something about them," Lady Ellan interrupted. "I mean, we can all communicate with Firestar. We know within ourselves that it is well but it must also know our concerns about the giants. Alarid only needs to *ask* to have the giants put back to sleep again, surely!"

Casimir pursed his lips. "Don't think I haven't been pushing for it," he sighed. "Believe me, I've tried a dozen times at least but nothing will shift him — and quite frankly, he's in charge. I can't override his authority any more than you can. He won't do a thing about the giants," he said grimly, "and that's that!"

Lord Rothlan frowned. "That's not like Alarid," he mused.

"The news isn't good, Alasdair. The ghosts say that the Americans are waiting for their satellite to make another strike and he can think of noth-ing else."

Lady Ellan clasped her husband's hand nerv-ously at this but her tone, when she spoke, was determined. "That doesn't mean that we should do nothing about the giants. They're causing complete havoc. Glens are impassable all over the Highlands."

"Something, somewhere must have triggered

the giants off, Casimir," Lord Rothlan pointed out. "They could never have risen on their own."

"The only thing of any importance that has happened is the attack on Firestar, Alasdair. It seems to have upset the old way of things completely."

"Hasn't anything shown up on the machine?" queried Lady Ellan.

"The machine was affected," Casimir said slowly. "Maybe we should go down and have a look at it. I had a chat with Rumbletop and he mentioned a strange icon on the monitor but as it doesn't seem to affect the machine, he's left it alone."

"Left it alone?" Lady Ellan echoed sharply. "Shouldn't he be doing something about it?"

"I think he's afraid to mess around with it," Casimir admitted. "Says he doesn't want to trigger another attack."

At this, Malfior, hidden in the depths of Firestar, smiled with ill-concealed glee and promptly communicated Casimir's feelings to Lord Jezail. His master, he knew, was pleased with all the little tit-bits of conversation that he passed on and he preened himself at his cleverness. Lord Rothlan, too, would soon be under his control and obviously hadn't the slightest suspicion that he was controlling the great Lords of the North. By focusing their fears on Firestar, he had quite successfully drawn their minds away from the threat of the giants. Indeed, if he was worried about anything at all it was that wretched icon. The last thing he wanted was the hobgoblins to access it on the machine and so far he'd succeeded in scaring the wits out them at the very thought. Apart from that, he reckoned, he was safe and in complete control. Why, even Firestar, the not-so-great power, hadn't a clue that he was there ...

"I might go down and have a look at that icon later on," Lord Rothlan frowned, settling back into his chair. "It must mean something, after all."

Casimir nodded. "Good idea," he said. "Oh, and talking of the hobgoblins reminds me — they told me some news that will interest you. It turns out that Neil and Clara are staying at Glenmorven House with Shona ... and Lewis is there, too."

Lady Ellan sat up. "Neil and Clara? In the glen? And Lewis! How lovely!"

"Do they know about the mountain?" queried Lord Rothlan. "I don't know that we ever mentioned it by name."

Prince Casimir smiled. "They must have their suspicions by this time," he said, "for they've already met a couple of our greedier hobgoblins. Apparently, they still scrounge cakes and biscuits from Hughie."

"They must be wearing their firestones, then," Lady Ellan observed.

The prince nodded in agreement. "Must be," he said, "for according to Hughie, they've seen Red Rory and the MacTavish."

Alasdair Rothlan raised his eyebrows and looked at him. "I thought you said the Americans had put the castle out of bounds?"

"Quite right," Casimir agreed, "but the children have been exploring the old secret passage that runs between the castle and Glenmorven House. The Fergusons still use it from time to time —

mostly when the weather's bad, I imagine. Shona shows it to all her friends."

"We owe a great deal to Neil and Clara — and Lewis, too, of course," added Lady Ellan hastily, meeting Casimir's eyes. "We really must invite them to meet the Lords of the North."

Lord Rothlan eyed his wife fondly. "I agree, Ellan," he said, "but this is hardly the time to land the Lords of the North with guests. Maybe later, when we've got Firestar sorted out."

"You're right, Alasdair," Prince Casimir said, fingering his firestone necklace thoughtfully. "I'm worried myself. I only hope that Tatler is having some success with the Americans. You know that he's trying to have them change the satellite's orbit."

Rothlan frowned. "Tatler knows his way round government circles both here and in the States," he said, "and I'm sure he'll do his best for us. But NASA, you know, can't be classed as 'government circles.' It's an organization in its own right with its own agenda. They mightn't listen to him."

As it happened, Lord Rothlan was correct in his assessment of the situation. Despite complaints from the British at Powerprobe's orbit, NASA officials had explained that, for technical reasons, it was quite impossible to comply with their wishes. And even as George Tatler lifted the telephone to call Sir James with the bad news, Powerprobe struck again.

23. Firestar strikes back

As Powerprobe locked on to Firestar, the Lords of the North felt themselves weaken and, eyeing one another apprehensively, grasped their firestones with trembling fingers. Lord Rothlan held Lady Ellan close and put his other arm protectively round Amgarad while Prince Casimir, sitting alone on his silver throne, gripped his hands together tightly and thought of his son.

Deep inside Morven, the hobgoblins froze as they felt the first slight tremor run through the machine. It had done it before and they knew what it signified. Another attack! Such was their fear that their tendrils positively blasted their way out of their heads and swirled round them. Rumbletop and Rumblegudgeon looked at one another in horror and made a concerted rush for the machine.

It was then that Rumblegudgeon tripped over his writhing tendrils and, with a yell of alarm, skated wildly across the marble floor to cannon violently into the control panel.

When word got round NASA that Powerprobe was due to lock on to Morven for a second time, an interested group of spectators gathered round Patrick Venner to watch the fun. Talk of the goat-faced alien had, of course, got round and, indeed, had generated much amusement. Most of the scientists regarded it as freak interference from a TV channel and poor Venner had been teased unmercifully about it ever since. After a while, he more than half-believed them himself and, being a good natured chap, took their teasing with as much good humour as he could muster.

Nevertheless, as he adjusted his monitor to receive the expected stream of data, he felt a sudden nervousness and, calling himself every sort of a fool under the sun, steadied a trembling hand and steeled himself for whatever might happen when Powerprobe locked, once more, on to Morven.

His fears, as it happened, were justified for the first thing the Americans saw on the monitor was Rumblegudgeon streaking towards them, his face displaying a variety of emotions. Alarm, fear and horror all registered as the little hobgoblin shot, shrieking, across the marble with the grace and speed of a twenty ton elephant slipping on a banana skin and as he'd no control over his flight whatsoever, it was hardly his fault that he landed up smack against the machine.

Venner's monitor picked the whole thing up. Hitherto sceptical NASA scientists grabbed at one another in panic as they saw Rumblegudgeon careering towards them, screaming fearsomely and as he grew ever larger, they ducked, as though expecting him to shoot straight through the screen and land in their midst. As it was, the final picture on the monitor gave them a pretty good view of his tonsils.

Predictably, chaos reigned supreme as everyone in the control room totally lost the plot.

Then Powerprobe's monitor went blank.

That shut everybody up.

As the babble of alarmed voices quietened abruptly, the horrified silence deepened, all eyes focusing on Pat Venner as he bent over his keyboard and tapped at it frantically. Apart from a single, dancing point of light, the monitor remained blank. He tried again and again to raise some kind of response from Powerprobe — any kind of response — but to no avail. He sat back in his chair with a sigh and, in a voice shaking with nerves, told everyone what they had already gathered.

"Sorry, guys," he said as a frisson of alarm rippled through the crowd, "but I reckon that Powerprobe's been zapped!"

Powerprobe had, indeed, been zapped.

Ever since the first attack, Firestar had been ripe for retaliation. As it had been in existence since more or less the beginning of time, it had a pretty fair working knowledge of the universe and although the original attack had taken it by surprise, causing it to miss the arrival of Malfior, the constituents of the lasers had by no means escaped its understanding.

So, as it happened, Firestar hadn't been at all disappointed when it felt the first tentative probing of the lasers. Indeed, it embraced them in much the same way as a spider welcomes a fly to its web; gladly and with a certain mouth-watering sense of anticipation. Once caught in its clutches, poor Powerprobe had as much chance of survival as a snowflake in hell.

With painstaking care, Firestar gathered together

every ounce of power it possessed and with a massive surge of blistering energy, shot a beam of light back through the lasers to Powerprobe and quite successfully zapped all of its computers.

The force of Firestar's assault not only shook Morven but rocked the entire glen. For an instant, the mountain became as clear as crystal with a bluish-white, vibrant core that shot in a stream of blazing light from the top of the mountain, through the sky and into the furthest reaches of the heavens. And, as the beam hung, suspended in the air, the wind picked it up in its arms so that its magic drifted over the land, houses and farms of Glenmorven and into the screes and corries of the surrounding glens.

Deep in the heart of the mountain, Firestar relaxed and breathed in its power once more. Scores had been settled and its charges, the Lords of the North and the peoples of the world of magic, could now live their lives in peace and safety to the days at the end of the world.

However, while Firestar swelled comfortably in satisfaction at a job well done, Malfior, curled in its depths, smiled nastily. It knew Firestar's mind and, indeed, it suited it that the connection to Powerprobe had been cut. Hidden and unsuspected, it could now grow unseen and unchecked.

24. Trapped

"There she is," Neil pointed in relief to a little scrap of a kitten that was scrambling frantically across the rough ground towards them.

"Ugly Mug!" Shona called. "Ugly Mug, We're coming!"

They all ran towards the kitten and Shona beamed happily as she scooped it up and cuddled it. "Are you hungry, then?" she crooned.

"She must be starving," Clara said, looking concerned, for Jennifer and her parents hadn't left Glenmorven until after lunch and it was now quite late in the afternoon.

The kitten miaowed plaintively. "We've brought you some food," Shona soothed, looking at Neil who'd pulled the lid off the can of cat food.

"She'll have to eat it out of the can," Neil said, bending down to let the kitten eat.

Ugly Mug wasn't fussy. She gobbled down the cat food until she could manage no more and then sat back to lick her paws and wash her face.

"Enough," Shona grinned, bending down to pick her up. Ugly Mug, however, seemed to think she was playing a game and by the time they caught her, it was later than Shona would have liked.

"We'll have to get a move on," she said, looking round. "It'll be dark soon."

Lewis zipped up his anorak and pulled the hood over his head as the wind gusted round them.

Then he stopped suddenly. "*What* was that?" he said, looking startled.

A strange noise, almost like an explosion, echoed round the glen and the ground shook under them. They looked at one another in alarm, thinking it was an earthquake until Shona looked up and pointed to the sky over the ridge. "Wow! Look at that! Morven's all lit up!"

Lewis, Neil and Clara eyed one another in astonishment. What was going on? This definitely looked like magic, and serious magic at that! They watched in awe as the great pillar of blue-white light that shot straight as an arrow into the sky, started to fade as the wind caught it and blew it in sweeping gusts towards them. As they made their way towards the ridge, they watched the sparkles of blue, glint in the wind and gradually fall to the ground until they were scattered here and there over the hillside, resting in the slopes around them. Soon there was nothing left to show that anything untoward had happened; the strange light faded and Morven reared in the distance, looking much the same as usual.

It was then that they heard a roaring from the glen behind them and, swinging round at the sudden sound of crashing rocks, saw that the slopes of the mountains were heaving with movement as giant shapes rose from the slopes and stretched stone limbs.

"The Cri'achan," Clara said, appalled. "They're rising from the mountains!"

"What are we going to do?" Shona gasped. "There ... there are so *many* of them!"

Jennifer's father had talked of there being three giants in the glen the night before but Neil reckoned at a quick glance that this time there must be ten or twelve at least. And they were huge. The newspapers had talked of giants the size of houses! These were more like blocks of flats!

"Run," Lewis gulped, "come on, run for the ridge!"

They didn't need to be told twice but when they turned to head for home, they saw, ahead of them, the rearing shapes of more giants.

"Do you think they are the same giants the Sinclairs saw yesterday?" Shona gasped, still clutching Ugly Mug.

Lewis looked round and turned pale as he realized that they were now cut off from Glenmorven. "We'll have to climb as high as we can," he gasped, "and maybe find a cave or something to shelter in until the giants pass. We can't stay here! We're right in their way!"

They started to run and, as they scrambled up the slopes, found to their amazement that they were covering the ground in huge leaps. Higher and higher they climbed until the top of the mountain was in sight. It was like being one of the men on the moon, Neil thought as he leapt effortlessly over a huge boulder and then struggled to keep his balance as he hit a steep slope on the other side. A corrie! Thank goodness! His eyes swept the cup-like hollow that nestled hidden on the side of the mountain.

"I've found a corrie," he shouted urgently, clambering up to the rim and waving his arms. "Quick!

Over here! It'll hide us from the giants!"

Still taking huge leaps, they headed towards him and piled into the hollow, collapsing in a heap against the rough grass and stones that formed its steep sides.

Neil, crouching behind its edge, peered down anxiously at the enormous giants that strode the valley floor. They were almost half as tall as the mountains themselves and as they marched along, their flailing arms knocked rocks and boulders from the sides of the mountains. They might not mean to harm anyone intentionally, he thought, but they could still do an enormous amount of damage to anyone standing in their way. He looked worriedly at Lewis who had climbed up beside him to scout out the lie of the land.

"We're still not safe," Neil muttered. "I don't know about you, but I'd give anything to be able to call a magic carpet."

Lewis smiled ruefully. They both knew that they were far too far away for their magic carpets to be of any use to them. "There's Casimir's ring," he whispered, so that Shona wouldn't hear him. "I could use it, couldn't I?" He held out his hand and they looked at the magic ring that Casimir had given him. "I've never used it before," he said doubtfully, "and I don't really know what would happen if I did. But this *is* an emergency, isn't it? I mean, we're completely surrounded."

Neil nodded and flinched as some of the giants moved closer to their part of the mountain.

Lewis ducked down below the rim of the corrie. "Casimir told me to rub it and call him if I needed help," he said, "and we certainly need it now."

"It means that we'll have to give the game away, though," Neil pointed out. "Shona doesn't know anything about our magic."

Lewis looked down at the two girls. "I know," he said, "but it's too dangerous to stay here. We can't go any further without the giants spotting us. We're trapped, Neil!"

Clara and Shona looked up at them anxiously as the giants' voices carried on the breeze. Only Neil, Clara and Lewis understood what they were saying, however, and Clara gripped her firestone tightly as the gravelly voices thundered and roared.

"Death to the Lords of Morven!" chanted the giants. "Death! Death!"

"That's it," Neil muttered, "go on, Lewis. You've no choice! You've got to tell the Lords of the North what's going on. Rub the ring! It's our only chance!"

Lewis held his right hand out, fingers spread, and looked at the strangely-formed ring with its design of interlocking snakes. *"Yasran,"* he said, experimentally, rubbing the metal gently and hoping fervently that he'd said the magic word properly. *"Yasran,"* he said again.

25. Court appearance

Even as Lewis said the magic word, the cold wind and the mountain disappeared and he felt a whirling, crushing feeling of blackness surround him. Just as he was beginning to wonder if it was ever going to stop, there was a sudden, warm surge of shimmering, comforting light. Tentatively, he opened his eyes, wondering where he had landed and what he might see. With magic, he thought worriedly, one just never knew. He hoped it wasn't a goblin's cave for a start. Of all the magic places he had visited in the past with Casimir, *that* had definitely been the worst.

The sight that met his eyes, however, was breathtaking in its beauty. He found himself staring in awe round the vast reaches of an elegant cavern whose lofty heights shone with a clear, blue-white light. A half circle of tall, silver thrones faced him and looking at the line-up of old, bearded figures that regarded him speculatively, he knew immediately where he was; for Prince Casimir had told him of the Court of the Lords of the North.

Feeling totally inadequate in old trainers, wet jeans and a scruffy anorak he walked towards the thrones and bowed so low that his head almost touched his knees.

"Welcome, Lewis," a familiar voice said, kindly. "Welcome to the Court of the Lords of the North."

Lewis straightened with a jerk, his eyes shining

with relief and affection as Prince Casimir rose from one of the thrones and came towards him, resplendent in robes of dull red velvet.

"We are delighted to see you, Lewis," Lady Ellan smiled as she came forward, followed by her husband. "You are most welcome."

"Well, Lewis," Lord Rothlan smiled understandingly. "Been getting up to mischief again, have you?"

Lewis almost blurted out the whole story there and then but experience had taught him to hold his tongue. He hadn't yet been introduced to the Lords of the North and that must come first. Casimir was a real stickler for proper behaviour.

The Lords of the North were particularly affable to Lewis and treated him with great kindness. Firestar, in its own inimitable fashion, had communicated the result of its actions to them and they were still dizzy with relief that the attacking power had been destroyed. Indeed, they had just been marvelling at their escape when Lewis had landed so unexpectedly in their midst.

Lewis, mindful of the fact that Casimir missed nothing, bowed low as he was introduced to each of the lords and was ushered by Lord Alarid, himself, to a chair by the low table where a crystal ball rested on an ebony stand.

"Now, Lewis," Prince Casimir said gravely as they took their seats round the table, "tell us your errand, for we know you wouldn't have come here without good reason."

Lewis, overawed despite himself, looked round the table at the expressions of polite enquiry on their faces. Lord Rothlan winked at him and, feeling heartened, he began his story. "Neil, Clara and I were in the next valley with Shona when ... when there was a sort of explosion and the mountains all shook. You ... you must have felt it ..." he looked at them doubtfully. "This *is* Morven, isn't it?"

Lord Rothlan nodded. "We did feel it, Lewis. And, yes, this *is* Morven. We'll tell you what happened later. Go on with your story."

"We saw a sort of bluish light shoot into the sky from Morven and as it fell back it seemed to spread over the whole area. I don't know if it was because of the light but stone giants suddenly rose from all the slopes around us. They're huge, twice as tall as houses, and we had to climb up the side of the mountain quickly to get out of their way. It was easy, though, for the magic dust seemed to have affected us as well — even Shona and *she* doesn't have a firestone. We could take huge steps and jump over high boulders without any effort at all."

The Lords of the North eyed one another anxiously. "The stone giants," Lord Alarid looked guiltily at Casimir. "I didn't know they had come so close to us."

"Neil and the girls are stuck on the side of Ben Garchory," Lewis added. "That's why I came to you, Prince Casimir. The giants were all around us, knocking boulders and stuff from the sides of the mountains. We were trapped. And ... well, that's why I came; so that you could rescue them."

Lord Alarid passed his hand over the glittering crystal and immediately the swirling mist cleared to show a huddled group of children crouched in a corrie near the top of the mountain. Then the view widened to reveal the length and breadth of Jennifer's glen. Lady Ellan gave a gasp of astonishment and her husband sat up in alarm, for the glen was full of enormous giants.

Malfior felt their dismay but this time was unable to influence their minds for the giants were there, in front of them, on the edge of Glenmorven itself.

Lord Alarid looked at each of the old lords in turn and, as they nodded, chanted the words of a hex. "They will not be able to enter," he said. "I have put a protective spell round the glen."

"And the children?" queried Lady Ellan anxiously.

Again the lords looked at one another.

"We could bring Neil and Clara in right away," Rothlan said, looking at Lewis enquiringly. "They *are* wearing their firestones, aren't they?"

Lewis nodded. "Yes, but Shona isn't."

"Arthur, I think," Casimir said thoughtfully. "The dragon will be able to stand up to the giants quite easily and the children can ride on his back."

"Better leave Neil and Clara where they are then," Lady Ellan said. "You'll need someone there to reassure Shona, otherwise she'll never go anywhere near Arthur."

"It's really urgent," Lewis looked at Casimir anxiously, "and Edinburgh's a long way away ..."

Lord Alarid passed a hand over the crystal so that it once again glowed to life.

"It's all right," Casimir assured him as the MacArthur's face appeared. "If Arthur uses a magic mirror, he can be here in seconds."

Lewis nodded and tried not to look disbelieving. He knew exactly how big Arthur was and the thought of the dragon squeezing its huge bulk through a magic mirror was mind-boggling. That, however, was exactly what happened. Everyone turned as one of the magic mirrors started to ripple. Arthur's head appeared followed by his neck, body, wings and tail, all of which expanded to their normal size in a burst of scarlet scales as he clawed his way through. The mirror rippled again as Archie and the MacArthur followed Arthur into the Great Hall and bowed low to the Lords of the North.

26. Arthur to the rescue

"Where's Lewis, Neil?" Shona demanded, looking round the corrie. "You were talking to him just a minute ago."

Neil glanced at Clara and looked uncomfortable. "He's gone to get help, Shona," he said. "He'll be back soon. Just hang on."

As Ugly Mug miaowed protestingly, Shona looked close to tears. "If he's found a way down the mountain then why couldn't we have gone with him?" she protested.

"Shhhh! Careful!" Neil hissed as one of the giants walked by quite close to them, its great feet crashing over rock and stone. Although it had no eyes, he could have sworn that its great head turned and looked at him. But the giant did nothing; it merely looked away again and strode purposefully on towards the head of the valley. All the giants seemed to be gathering there and Neil paled at the thought of them crossing the ridge and heading for Morven.

"I hope they don't cause a landslide," Clara whispered, pressing her back against the rocky wall of the corrie, "for that's our only way into Glenmorven."

Shona, however, was not to be diverted. Once the giant had passed she persisted. "I didn't see Lewis leave," she hissed. "He just seemed to disappear!"

Clara gave up. "Actually," she said, with a quick glance at Neil, "he did disappear."

"Clara," Neil said warningly.

"He has a magic ring," Clara said, "and he rubbed it so that he could bring us help."

Shona looked at her in disbelief. "A magic ring?" She repeated, her eyes round. "Are you nuts or something?"

Clara took a deep breath. "Actually, Neil and I have magic rings as well. Watch!" Clara changed her ring over to the other hand and immediately disappeared.

Shona's mouth fell open but before she could say anything, Clara switched the ring back to her other hand and reappeared. "Want me to do it again?" she asked with a grin.

"I don't believe you just did that," Shona gasped. "I mean ... it isn't possible!"

"Yes it is," Neil smiled. "Just watch me!" And he promptly did the same.

Clara smiled reassuringly. "It's okay, Shona," she said. "I know it takes some believing but the fact is that we both have magic rings that can make us invisible."

Shona still looked white. "What are you?" she asked.

Neil burst out laughing. "Cool it, Shona," he smiled, "we're not aliens or anything."

Shona looked nervously from one to the other, still unconvinced.

"Okay, then. Just tell me — why, exactly, are we hiding here?" Neil asked.

Shona glanced fearfully towards the glen. "We're ... we're hiding from the giants," she admitted.

"And aren't giants magic?" Clara asked.

"Yes, but ... but that's all folk tales and legends. Hughie's a great one for stories about kelpies and the like ... but nobody really believes in magic. I mean," she eyed the giants doubtfully, "they look solid enough but ..."

They turned their heads in alarm as there was a sudden, great noise from the far end of the glen where the giants now seemed to be milling around angrily. Neil counted fourteen in all and wondered worriedly what was going on. Although he didn't realize it, the protective shield set by the Lords of the North had slid into place just in time. It stopped the giants in their tracks and try as they might, they found to their dismay that they couldn't get into Glenmorven.

The noise was tremendous as they heaved their weight again and again against the protective shield and, in their anger at finding their way so efficiently barred, many of them started to lash out at the mountains with great stone arms. Some turned and began to walk back the way they'd come but they were no longer the peaceful figures of before. They were now furiously angry and, as they stomped their way along, they thumped furiously at rock, cliff and crag; anything that stood in their way.

"If you think about it, Shona, magic's the only explanation," Neil remarked. "As I said, if it isn't magic then what are we doing here on the side of Ben Garchary, hiding from giants? It's not a dream, is it?"

Shona peered through the gathering darkness at the crowd of giants that were still clomping and clattering around at the head of the glen. "It has to be a dream," she said in a very small, scared voice. "It has to be a dream because I can see a dragon flying towards us."

Neil and Clara jerked round and saw, not only a dragon flying towards them but, soaring above it, the winged shape of a great eagle.

"Arthur," Neil gasped. "He's come to rescue us!"

"Amgarad!" Clara's eyes shone with delight. "Amgarad as well!" she said, excitedly. "What do you bet that Lord Rothlan's in Morven!"

Shona shrank back, petrified, and dropping the tiny kitten, opened her mouth and let out an ear-splitting shriek as the huge, winged shape of the enormous dragon swooped over the mountains towards them.

"For goodness sake, grab the cat, Clara," Neil said urgently. And, as Clara scooped up a dazed Ugly Mug from the heather, Neil jumped on top of a boulder, waved his arms wildly and yelled "Arthur!" at the top of his voice.

Clara stuffed the frightened kitten down the front of her anorak and tightened the cord round the waist, hoping that the kitten wouldn't try and scratch her way out. Ugly Mug, however, was not unintelligent. She much preferred the warmth and safety of Clara's anorak to being carried in a bouncing bag and promptly settled herself comfortably in the folds of her sweater.

"Amgarad," Clara said in delight as the great eagle flew down beside her. "Did Lewis tell you that we were here?"

The eagle settled his wings and nodded majestically. "Prince Casimir summoned Arthur to rescue you."

"Amgarad," Neil called in sudden dismay, "come and look, quick! The giants are attacking Arthur! And, gosh, Archie's on his back!"

Actually, the giants had had it in for Arthur from the start. Why, Neil didn't know, although Arthur told him later that it was a centuries-old hatred that had never died. He himself had forgotten the reason for it and so, probably, had the giants. But there it was. The minute they spotted him, there was complete and utter pandemonium.

Fourteen enormous giants on the rampage was a breathtaking sight. Despite their size and clumsy movements, they entered into the spirit of battle with a wild determination that bordered on enthusiasm; grabbing rocks from the sides of the mountains and happily slinging anything and everything they could lay their hands on, at the dragon. Fortunately for Arthur, the giants were, to put it mildly, rotten shots — but the hail of largely unguided missiles that were sailing through the air was, nevertheless, impressive. Arthur's magic, however, protected him and even when it seemed that a lucky shot would most certainly hit him, the rock was somehow deflected and fell harmlessly to one side.

The realization that nothing seemed to be hitting the dragon, spurred the giants to greater efforts and, as the hail of rocks and stones grew heavier, Arthur was forced to veer away from the children, in case they were hit.

Shona couldn't believe her eyes as she watched

Neil and Clara clutch at one another in anxiety as the dragon was pelted with rocks. And how come Clara seemed to be able to talk to an eagle? The fearsome bird was perched beside her, hissing angrily at the giants as they lobbed huge rocks around like so much confetti.

Again Arthur's magic came into play. Neil and Clara didn't realize it at the time and, for a few minutes, their hearts sank at the thought that the giants might be winning; for before their startled eyes, the stone figures started to grow. Indeed, Clara put her hand over her mouth to stop herself from crying out in horror as she watched them shoot up until they were the height of skyscrapers. As they grew taller and taller, however, they also became thinner and thinner until they were little more than huge, rickety skeletons of rock and stone.

It didn't take the giants long to realize the dangers of such unexpected growth and they roared with rage as the magic spell took hold. Indeed, they promptly forgot about Arthur as the need to keep their balance became paramount. Now disastrously unstable, many of the giants grabbed at cliffs for support as they started to sway dangerously.

Arthur hissed in satisfaction as the giants' faltering steps became more and more perilous and swept towards the mountain top in a blaze of fire and smoke. He landed, wings outspread, on a jutting spur of rock, his wonderful eyes gleaming with excitement.

"Come on, Neil," he hissed in his dragon's voice, "let's get you out of here!"

Clambering awkwardly down from the spur of rock towards them, Arthur blew a triumphant stream of sparkling fire. Neil and Clara were quite used to what they termed 'Arthur's fireworks' but Shona was understandably terrified of the great red dragon that was only feet from them. She clutched frantically at Neil as the dragon blew another stream of sparkling, glittering fire.

"Don't *do* that, Arthur! You're scaring Shona," Clara said, rushing forward to hug him.

"Hi, Arthur! Hi Archie!" Neil grinned as Archie slipped down from Arthur's back. "It's great to see you! Come and meet Shona."

Shona looked at Archie in fascinated wonder as he bowed to her and gave her a reassuring grin, knowing that it wasn't every day that she met faery folk. When Amgarad spread his wings, however, she looked more than a bit apprehensive and turned to Neil fearfully.

"Look, there's no time to explain right now," Neil said, seeing the confused mixture of horror and disbelief on her face, "but it's all magic. Archie is magic, the dragon is magic and so is Amgarad."

"Come and meet Arthur, Shona," Clara said, tugging her hand. "He's really not the least bit terrifying when you know him. He's fabulous. Look at his wonderful eyes. He's come to rescue us!"

Shona was quite definite about it. "I am not," she said determinedly, "I am not getting on that dragon."

Clara glanced up at Arthur. He did, she supposed, look quite fearsome. He was huge for a start and the swirling clouds of dust that the giants had kicked up made him look exciting, mysterious and ... well, she could understand how Shona felt.

"Neil's flown on him before, Shona," she said encouragingly, "and he loved every minute of it. Arthur's a lovely dragon. He's our friend and he won't hurt you, I promise."

It was one of the giants that eventually persuaded Shona that it was safer to climb onto Arthur's back with the others than stay where she was. One giant had grown so tall that his head was more or less on a level with them and as the rocky, eyeless head appeared above the rim of the corrie, Shona gave a yell of fright.

"Here, take my hand, Shona," Neil said, "and I'll help you up onto Arthur's back. Clara, you go first."

Arthur dropped his wing obligingly so that Clara could clamber up and perch behind his neck; then Shona, too, scrambled up and settled herself behind Clara, her arms clutching her tightly round the waist.

As Neil climbed up behind her, Archie then ran up to Amgarad and Shona's eyes widened as he seemed to melt into the great eagle. Clara, however, hid a smile as she, too, watched Archie merge with the enormous bird; for poor Archie was more accustomed to merging with humble pigeons and it had long been his ambition to merge with an eagle. Now, at last, he had his wish and she was happy for him. She watched as Amgarad's wings flapped strongly and, with effortless ease, he soared upwards over the top of the mountain.

"Archie's merged with an eagle at last," she said, turning to look at Neil whose eyes were following Amgarad's flight enviously.

Arthur flapped his wings as Amgarad soared into the sky. "Our turn next," Neil said, warningly. "Hang on everyone!"

Instinctively, they gripped Arthur's sides with their knees, clinging tightly to one another as Arthur blew a stream of fire and smoke, flapped his great wings and soared effortlessly into the sky.

In the last rays of the setting sun, they could see where he was heading, for the mountain stood sharply outlined against the night sky. Like Amgarad, Arthur was making for Morven.

27. Inside Morven

Shona looked down as they soared over the mountain top and as the glen unfolded beneath them, her eyes searched the gathering gloom to see if she could see signs of torchlight. Her parents, she knew, must be worried about them.

"You all right, Shona?" Neil asked.

She nodded her head. "I'm fine," she said with a grin. "It's because I can't believe it's happening," she admitted. "I just know I'm in a dream. How can I be flying on a dragon's back? It's impossible."

Neil smiled, glad that she had relaxed, and as they drew nearer to Morven, pointed out Glenmorven House and Hughie's cottage. He frowned in sudden alarm as he had expected Arthur to land somewhere close by so that they could get home quickly and reassure the Fergusons that they were quite safe. Arthur, however, didn't seem to be losing height at all and, instead of landing, they passed over Glenmorven House. It was then that they realized he was heading for Morven, itself. He wasn't slowing down either and as the mountain loomed large in front of them, Neil gave a sudden yell of alarm. "Arthur, slow down! We're going to hit the mountain!"

"Amgarad!" Clara yelled, her eyes frantic with shock. "Amgarad, look out!" For the great bird was swooping at speed towards the rocky sides of the mountain. Clara hardly dared look. She was sure he was going to hit it. "Amgarad! Nooooo!" she cried.

Amgarad didn't exactly *hit* the mountain; he seemed to disappear through it.

Neil cottoned on immediately to what was happening. "We're going to do the same," Neil shouted as the girls started to scream. "Hold on tight! We're going ... throuuuuuuuugh!"

There was no impact. They flew clean through the rocky slopes without feeling a thing and their screams tailed off as they realized that they were quite safe and flying through a vast, brightly lit cavern inside the mountain. At last, Shona thought, looking around in wonder. At last I'm inside the mountain. I always thought there was something magic about it and now I'm going to find out what it is. Peering over Clara's shoulder she could see a raised dais at the far end of the hall, where high-backed, silver thrones curved in a wide half circle.

Arthur's claws slid and slithered over the polished expanse of cream-coloured marble and as he came to a somewhat undignified halt in front of the thrones, a tall, white-haired old man rose and moved towards him. Arthur sank to his knees and bowed low.

Lord Alarid touched his head. "Well done, Arthur," he said gently. "We were wise to ask you to rescue the children." He looked at them, smiling at the amazement on their faces. "Welcome," he said, "welcome to the Court of the Lords of the North."

Formal introductions were then made and

Lewis's lips twitched in a smile as he saw the wonder on Shona's face as they met the gloriously robed magicians.

"Shona," Lord Alarid said, kindly, "we are pleased to meet you at last. We have watched you grow up over the years and know that you love Morven."

"I ... I've always felt it was a special mountain," Shona admitted, shyly, "but until now I didn't know how special. It's ... it's wonderful!"

Neil, meanwhile, scanned the hall and breathed a sigh of relief as he saw Archie, who had obviously demerged safely from Amgarad, talking to Lewis and the MacArthur at the side of the dais. Thank goodness, Lewis was okay.

Standing tall and impressive to one side of the dais was a magic mirror. Neil eyed it almost fondly. Magic mirrors had played a large part in their lives and were powerful objects of magic. So, thought Neil, that's how Arthur and Archie had appeared so quickly to rescue them. They must have come from Edinburgh through the mirrors. Amgarad, he noticed, had already flown to perch on the arm of Lord Rothlan's throne and spread his wings in greeting as they approached. All the lords were present and as they bowed their way along the line, Lord Rothlan and Lady Ellan rose and hugged them warmly, as did Prince Casimir.

Shona, who still half-believed she was in a dream, eyed them in amazement and some wonder. The magicians; for they must be magicians, Shona reckoned, seemed absolutely delighted to see Neil and Clara and obviously knew them well.

Ugly Mug caused a stir when she jumped down onto the floor and, seeing Shona, pranced happily towards her. Then she saw the dragon and her fur stood on end in tiny spikes as she backed off, hissing and spitting furiously. Arthur, however, batted his wonderful eyes at the kitten and as Clara bent to pick her up, a stream of magic comforted the little creature.

"Lewis has been telling me about the stone giants, Neil," Lord Rothlan said. "You mustn't worry, you know. The old lords have put a protective shield round Glenmorven so they won't be able to get in."

"Why are they so anxious to get into the glen, Lord Rothlan?" Clara asked. "Do they want to come to the mountain?"

"We don't know the reason, Clara," Rothlan answered. "We think the first attack released them from Firestar's spell but we don't know why they want to come here."

"We heard about Firestar from Hughie," nodded Neil. "Was that the explosion that shot through the top of the mountain?"

Rothlan nodded. "Firestar was ready for the second attack. It wouldn't let itself be caught out a second time."

Clara suddenly grabbed Neil's arm. "Look," she whispered, "look, Neil, over there. There are some of the little creatures we saw on the hill."

"We call them the Rumblegrumbles," Lady Ellan said with a smile as she saw their heads turn. "They look after Firestar and the Lords of the North."

"Their hair sort of grew when we saw them," Clara frowned at the memory.

"It depends on how anxious they are," Prince Casimir said, looking amused. He beckoned to the hobgoblins and as they trotted over in their waist-coats and flappy trousers, looking shy, he smiled at them reassuringly.

"When they're really worried you can hardly see them for tendrils!" Lady Ellan whispered.

"This is Rumbletop and Rumbletumble," Casimir said. The hobgoblins shifted on their little hooves, tugged at their waistcoats and bowed.

"We saw you on the mountain, didn't we?" Clara said, crouching down to be at their level.

There was a nodding of heads and funny little grins as the hobgoblins pulled their lips back from their front teeth in winsome smiles that made them look totally idiotic and absolutely charming.

Then they saw Shona and ran up to her, pulling at her jeans and jumping up and down. "Shona, this is wonderful! *You* can see us now, *too*!"

"As well as who?" Shona laughed.

"As well as Hughie," Rumbletop said, his yellow eyes shining as the other hobgoblins gathered round her excitedly.

"Hughie?" Shona sounded startled. "*Hughie* can see you? He ... he never told me!"

Rumbletop's grin faded at the note of dismay in Shona's voice and as all the hobgoblins' tendrils started to sprout, he looked at Prince Casimir in consternation.

Lady Ellan, seeing Shona's distress, put an arm round her shoulders. "Hughie found his way into

Morven when he was a boy," she consoled her, "a bit like Neil and Clara going into Arthur's Seat. He's always loved the Rumblegrumbles and they still visit him."

"I'm sure he must have *wanted* to tell you about them, Shona," Lord Rothlan added, "but I'm afraid we'd sworn him to secrecy long before you were born."

"Oh," Shona said in tones of relief, "that's all right, then. He couldn't break his word, could he?"

"No, he couldn't," Lady Ellan smiled, glad that the matter was resolved.

As the hobgoblins fussed happily round Shona, Clara whispered to Neil. "It's fantastic here, Neil, but what about the Fergusons? They'll be out of their minds with worry by this time."

Lady Ellan heard her and shook her head. "Don't worry, Clara," she said. "You know that our time is different from yours and although it might feel as though you've spent hours with us, none of your time will have passed at all. When you get home, you'll find that the Fergusons won't have missed you."

"They're going to ask lots of questions, though," Lewis pointed out. "They must have heard the explosion from the mountain and seen the stream of light from the top."

Lord Rothlan shook his head. "I think you'll find that no one in the glen will remember what happened today."

"We've put a magic spell on the glen," Lady Ellan smiled, seeing Shona's startled face, "and talking of magic ... ," she unfastened a velvet bag that hung at her waist and drew out a firestone, "you are going to need this to leave the mountain."

"Firestones," Lewis said, pulling on the thin gold chain so that Shona could see the amber stone that hung round his neck.

"Neil, Clara and Lewis all have firestones," smiled Lady Ellan, "and I'm sure they'll tell you all about them when you get home. This is yours," she said, handing Shona a chain with a firestone threaded through it. "Please guard it well."

Shona looked at the magic stone in awe. "It seems to have a light in the middle," she said.

"That's part of Arthur's fire," Neil explained. "That's why they're called firestones."

When they had once again thanked the Lords of the North and Arthur and Amgarad for their rescue, Lady Ellan told them to join hands in a circle. Then, straightening her arm, she'd murmured the words of a spell and, in an instant, they found themselves in the garden of Glenmorven House.

Helen Ferguson looked up with a smile as they trooped into the kitchen, suddenly realizing that they were ravenously hungry.

"Did you get the kitten, Shona?" she asked.

Shona nodded and held out a drowsy little cat who had had quite enough excitement for one day.

"I thought you said she was ugly?" she queried. "She's beautiful. A bit of Persian in there somewhere, I should say."

Clara looked at Ugly Mug closely. "Gosh, she is pretty! Look at her!"

"Jennifer won't be able to call her Ugly Mug any more," Lewis laughed, "not with a face like that."

After an enormous dinner, they all trooped into the garden. Shona could hardly believe it had all happened. The only thing that proved she wasn't dreaming was the beautiful firestone that hung round her neck. She looked at it again and saw the glint of dragon fire that lurked in its amber depths.

"Come on," she said, "let's visit Hughie! I want him to know that we can see the hobgoblins too! He'll be really pleased."

28. Prince Kalman returns

Resting gratefully on the crest of a ridge, its body quivering with fatigue, the great stag was almost spent. Kalman, equally exhausted, suffered with it. Several of the huge rocks that the giants had thrown at them in the course of their frantic flight had, more by luck than design, managed to hit home. Indeed, the result would have been little short of disastrous had it not been for his magic. Even then, the stag was a sorry sight; blood ran down the side of its face from a deep gash, one of its hind legs dragged awkwardly and broken antlers hung crazily over its neck.

Ever since he'd left Kenny, Larry and the van, the giants had been after him, rising from the mountains when he'd least expected it and all the time trying to force him over mountain tops and through glens that would have led him away from Morven. Eventually, he'd managed to give them the slip but the rumble of noise from the next glen told him that they were still far too close for comfort.

Nevertheless, his heart swelled in relief as he looked through the stag's brown eyes at the homely, familiar shape of the mountain that reared before them. Morven! He could hardly believe it! They'd made it at last!

His eyes scanned the valley anxiously. No giants so far, he thought, his eyes resting on the towers of Morven Castle, the white gleam of the Ferguson's house and the sweep of trees round Hughie's cottage, tucked in the shelter of a sloping bank.

It was then that he saw Amgarad swooping through the air towards the mountain. His eyes widened in surprise as he followed the bird's flight. Amgarad! That must mean that Lord Rothlan was in Morven, for the bird rarely left him. His spirits rose at the thought for much as he disliked him, Rothlan, unlike Lord Alarid and the other doddering old lords, was decisive, competent and efficient. If Alasdair Rothlan were there, then there was a chance that Firestar could be saved. Suddenly, the distinctive shape of a dragon appeared out of the gathering gloom. Arthur, the prince thought. He was obviously following Amgarad and also bound for Morven. Now what was *he* doing so far north — and who was he carrying? He could see that there were children on his back and his lips twisted grimly as he guessed that Neil and Clara were probably amongst them. But who was the other one? He counted at least three and looked decidedly puzzled as he watched the eagle and the dragon disappear into the slopes of the mountain.

The knowledge that Rothlan was in Morven, however, gave his spirits the lift they needed. Not long now, Kalman assured the stag as it picked its way towards Hughie's cottage. Keep going, just a little further ... just keep going ...

By the time they reached the cottage, the stag was barely able to walk but it knew instinctively that come what may, it had to reach the slopes of the mountain. Wearily, Kalman led its footsteps round the side of the little house to the foot of the towering peak and as the beast collapsed in the heather, Firestar's magic reached out to it and gave it comfort.

Hughie, who had caught sight of the stag from his kitchen window, watched in wonder as a familiar figure demerged from its back. He stiffened in amazement. Surely it was Prince Kalman, he thought. It was years since he'd last seen him but there was no mistaking the long fair hair and clean-cut features. Instead of making his way to the cottage as Hughie expected, however, Kalman threw himself flat on the heather beside the stag, his arms outstretched and his face hard against the earth.

Firestar immediately responded to his need and greedily he absorbed its magic until he could hold no more. His eyes closed in relief and his heart sang; to have his power back, to be strong again; for an instant, tears clouded his eyes at the wonder of it. Thankfully, he breathed in the fresh smell of the earth and would have lain longer had the stag beside him not scrambled to its feet. He, too, rose and reaching out to the stag, drew it towards him and murmured the words of a hex. At the touch of his fingers the wound on its face healed, the broken antlers righted themselves and its injured leg straightened; in little more than a few seconds, it was whole again. Knowing the threat of the hunter's gun, Kalman also put a protective shield round it. After the perils of their journey, he thought, it was the least he could do and he raised his hand in salute, watching with a half smile as the great beast tossed its head in thanks and turned to the slopes of the mountain.

As the stag made its way upwards over the heather and rough grass, Kalman, for an instant, stood straight and tall. Stretching out his arms, he used his new-found magic to cast another hex. It was a powerful hex and, under normal circumstances, should have taken him straight into the Court of the Lords of the North. Nothing, however, happened. He gave a curious, twisted smile. Firestar might have restored his magic but it would not admit him to Morven. He was still an outcast.

Hughie opened the kitchen door and waited as the prince turned and made his way towards him.

"Prince Kalman!" he said curiously, "are you all right?"

Kalman nodded. "I'm fine," he said tiredly, "but you'll have to hide me, Hughie. There are giants after me."

"And the stag?" Hughie's gaze lifted towards the mountain.

"He'll be all right," Kalman assured him. "He's a fine animal. He's brought me all the way from Argyll ..."

"Argyll?" Hughie echoed in amazement, knowing the length of their journey.

"We travelled in a van part of the way," Kalman admitted, "with a couple of youngsters who called themselves the Jelly Beans." He smiled wryly. "They fancied themselves as pop stars."

"That wouldn't be Kenny and Larry, would it?" Hughie looked at him in surprise. "The radio's been broadcasting nothing else. They were chased by giants and had their van smashed up. They're real heroes, the pair of them!"

Kalman almost smiled. "Nothing would have happened to them, Hughie, I made sure of that, but yes, in another way, they are real heroes."

Hughie looked at the prince anxiously as he made his way into the long, low kitchen and collapsed into an armchair by the fire, relaxing in its warmth.

"I was just going to have supper," Hughie offered, eyeing him questioningly. "I'll lay another place, shall I?"

Kalman nodded. "Actually, I'm starving," he admitted.

It was only when the prince had finished eating that Hughie ventured a question. "What happened?" he asked. "May I know?"

Kalman gave a twisted smile. "Firestar is in danger, Hughie," he said, "I've come to warn Lord Alarid."

Hughie looked at him doubtfully. The hobgoblins were a gossipy lot and always kept him up to date on the affairs of the Lords of the North. He knew perfectly well that Prince Kalman ranked as an outcast. However, it wouldn't do to say so. "Morven sort of exploded this afternoon," he said slowly, "did you know?"

"I felt it," Kalman said, wincing at the thought.

"I haven't seen Rumbletop to find out what happened," Hughie admitted.

"There's a lot going on in Morven that they don't know about, Hughie," Kalman rose from the chair and paced the floor. "I *must* get a message through to Alarid and warn him of his danger."

"But I thought ..." Hughie broke off uncertainly.

"The message I carry to the Lords of the North is more important than my quarrel with them."

"I still don't understand. Why can't you just magic yourself into the mountain?"

Kalman's eyes dropped. "I tried," he admitted, his face flushing. "I tried, but the mountain wouldn't let me in," he said. "You must know that the Lords of the North cast me out and my father and I ..." he tailed off, "we don't speak to one another any more."

"It might not be that," Hughie said, frowning. "Rumblegudgeon told me that Lord Alarid has put a protective shield round Morven."

"A protective shield wouldn't keep me out, Hughie. I'm still a Lord of the North. Was it put in place to keep out the giants?"

"No ... yes ... at least, I don't think so. Jamie Robertson let the castle to some Americans and ever since they've been here, they've been trying to get into the mountain. So Lord Alarid put a shield round it."

The prince looked vaguely surprised at the mention of Americans but dismissed them from his mind as he concentrated on the matter in hand. "I'm banking on *you* now, Hughie," he said. "*You* got into the mountain as a boy and there was no magic in you when you appeared before us all those years ago. I want *you* to take my message into the hill. Is the way still open? Could you do it, do you think?"

Hughie knew that he couldn't refuse. Come what may, he had to try although his heart sank within him at the thought of the desperately dangerous route he'd taken as a youngster — for without the strength of youth, he doubted if he'd manage the passages, ravines and sheer cliffs that lay inside the mountain. "Of course, I'll go," he said reassuringly, "but I'm an old man now, Prince Kalman and there's little strength left in me. I'd probably need some of your magic to help me through."

The prince shook his head. "I'm afraid my magic wouldn't help you," he said stiffly. "Not the way things are at the moment."

Hughie looked downcast but then his eyes brightened. "If all you want is a message passed on to the old lords, wouldn't it be easier if you just gave it to Rumbletop or one of the other hobgoblins?"

"I could do that, I suppose," Kalman mused, considering the option.

It was at this moment that the door burst open and Shona ran into the room followed by Lewis, Neil and Clara.

"Hughie," Shona cried, "we've just been inside the mountain and Lord Rothlan told us that ... that you ..." she paused at the sight of the gorgeously attired prince who had swung round sharply as she'd entered. He now stood rigid, his face a frozen mask but his eyes hooded as they looked beyond her and met those of Neil and Clara. There was a deathly silence.

"Prince Kalman!" Clara gasped.

29. Kalman's tale

Hughie looked from Prince Kalman to the frightened faces of the children. That they could see the prince at all came as a shock to him but that they should be afraid of him was little short of astounding.

"What's all this?" he asked, startled. "Do you know the prince?"

"I'll deal with this, Hughie," Kalman said stiffly. "Neil, Clara, please sit down," he commanded, gesturing to Hughie's worn but comfortable arm-chairs.

Shona looked at Hughie doubtfully. "Do you want us to go, Hughie?"

"No," the prince ordered, "you will stay." He looked at Neil. "Who are your friends, Neil? And how can they see me?"

"We were in Morven this afternoon," Neil answered. "Lady Ellan gave Shona a firestone. Lewis already has one."

Lewis bowed to the prince. "I'm pleased to meet you at last, Prince Kalman," he said evenly. "Your father told me about you."

Kalman raised his eyebrows. "Did he indeed," he said, disdainfully.

Lewis felt such a rush of anger that his eyes blazed furiously. Hughie took one look at his face and, grabbing his arm, pushed him into a chair. "Save your arguments for later," he advised, "there are more important things afoot at the moment."

Neil and Clara perched nervously on the edge of

their chairs while Shona sat down on the settee, looking round-eyed at Prince Kalman. The prince, Clara thought, looked ill. He was still as arrogant as ever but his robes were stained in places and torn round the hem. As she had never seen him in clothes that were anything less than immaculate she knew that whatever had happened, he hadn't come out of it well.

In a swirl of velvet, the prince moved in front of the fire as though drawing comfort from its warmth and looked at them.

"I need your help," he said abruptly.

Neil looked thunderstruck. This was the last thing he had expected to hear from the lips of the prince. "*You!*" he said in startled amazement, "*you* need *our* help?"

Kalman frowned and shot a glance at Hughie.

"I think Prince Kalman would like you to deliver a message," Hughie said, "to the Lords of the North."

There was a silence. It was Clara who broke it. "But ... you *are* a Lord of the North, Prince Kalman," she said, her face puzzled. "Why do you need us to help you?"

"Morven is forbidden to me," the prince said shortly, "but you can enter. You're wearing your firestones, aren't you?"

Neil and Clara nodded.

"You say you've just been in the hill," the prince continued. "You must know that there have been two attacks on Firestar." He looked directly at Neil. "Morven is in great danger," the prince said. "There is a new force in the world of magic. It is hidden inside Firestar and is feeding on its power. The Cri'achan are its friends."

"The giants!" Clara gasped.

"They're your friends, too, milord," Neil pointed out, remembering how Kalman had raised the Old Man of the Mountains against them in Hell's Glen.

The prince smiled sourly. "They *were* my friends," he admitted, "but they have turned against me. This new wizard, this Malfior," he almost spat the word out, "has promised them many things." He gestured vaguely. "Instead of being tied to the mountains, unable to move, he has returned them to their old way of life. You must have heard that they're able to walk freely through the glens. Not only that, he has promised Cri'achan Mòr a new, wonderful home for the giants in the halls of Morven. That's why they're on the move; they've come to claim Morven as their own."

There was a stunned silence. Everyone believed the prince implicitly and were horrified at his words.

"That's ... that's awful!" Neil said. "The Lords of the North think they're safe!"

The prince inclined his head. "That is the message I wish you to take to Lord Alarid," he said. His lips twisted in a rueful smile. "And you can also tell Alasdair Rothlan that I am relying on him to rid Firestar of this Malfior."

Neil and Clara looked at one another doubtfully. "The thing is," Neil said, "we didn't get into the mountain by ourselves. Arthur took us there. Couldn't you magic us in?"

Kalman shook his head. "No," he muttered. "No, I can't."

It was then that Lewis muttered the magic word. *"Yasran,"* he said softly as he rubbed his ring and disappeared.

Hughie started in amazement as Lewis suddenly vanished into thin air, Shona jumped up from the settee in alarm. Neil glanced at Clara in relief, however, knowing that Lewis must have gone to bring Prince Casimir. Much the best thing, he thought.

Kalman swung round and even as his glance focused on the empty chair, his father appeared with Lewis beside him.

Prince Casimir's relief at seeing his son safe and well was momentary as he took in, not only the shabbiness of his attire, but also the drawn, haggard lines of strain that marked his face. What on earth, he wondered anxiously, had Kalman been up to, to get himself into such a state?

The prince, seeing at a glance that his father was fit and well, turned his attention to Lewis. Who was this boy to have such magic power? It was only when his eyes dropped to the ring of intertwining gold snakes on Lewis's finger that realization dawned and its significance hit him like a blow. His father must have given him the ring!

The prince gave Lewis the oddest of looks. Disbelief and sheer fury vied for expression as his eyes flew from his father to the black-haired boy that stood at his side. If looks could kill, thought Clara tensely, Lewis would be very dead — for the feeling of antagonism that shot between them was almost palpable.

Kalman's jealous, thought Neil, appreciating for the first time the amount of power that Casimir had given Lewis. His magic ring had far more power in it than any firestone.

Casimir, too, sensed his son's jealousy and eyed him warily. "Lewis tells me that you have something very important to tell me, Kalman," he said evenly.

Kalman clenched his hands and tried to control his feelings, amazed at the wave of hatred that he felt for Lewis. Until that moment he hadn't realized just how much his father meant to him — and the knowledge that he thought enough of a human boy to give him a ring of power, was devastating. "I'm glad you're here, milord," he said, bowing abruptly to his father. "There's a lot I have to tell you and I'm afraid it's all bad news."

"Perhaps you should sit down, Prince Casimir," Hughie said hurriedly, trying to break the tension. He drew an armchair forward for the prince and there, in the humble surroundings of Hughie's kitchen, they listened to Kalman's tale of the giants' cavern under the mountains in Hell's Glen and of Malfior, the malevolent power that lurked within Firestar.

"It spoke to me," Kalman said, pacing the floor, "and laughed because it thought it had me trapped. Its hold on the giants is strong for the evil, yellow light that shone from the face of Cri'achan Mòr was that of a ferocious, grasping intelligence. Luckily, I'd seen two of the stone giants in the glen before I went into the mountain and, well, it had crossed my mind that maybe the Cri'achan wouldn't be quite as friendly as they'd been in the past. I cast a spell that would return me to the body of the stag should I be attacked and it's just as well that I did. The moment Malfior attacked me, I vanished, but in that crucial few seconds he managed to strip me of most of my magic power."

Casimir looked at him in amazement and gave a murmur of dismay. This was totally unexpected and much worse than anything he'd ever envisaged. If the prince's magic power had been taken from him that easily then it could certainly happen to the rest of the Lords of Morven.

"Travelling in the body of the stag was slow but fortunately I met up with two musicians who had a van. They drove me most of the way to Morven."

Neil and Clara looked at one another and knew immediately who he meant, for the Jelly Beans had made the headlines in all the newspapers. Neil made a mental note to read the interviews more closely as he was quite sure that there hadn't been any mention of a stag.

"This evening," the prince continued, "I arrived here and was able to renew my power from Firestar." He paused, looking at his father grimly. "Malfior will know this and he will know that I am here. Now, he'll be waiting for you to try to find him and will bury himself even deeper inside Firestar. He'll also call the giants to attack the mountain."

"They won't be able to get in," Casimir assured him. "The Lords of the North have put a protective shield round Morven."

"That's something," Kalman acknowledged,

"but what's even more important is that you find a way to get rid of Malfior. The machine must surely be able to give you some indication of its existence?"

Prince Casimir looked serious. "I rather think I know what it is," he said grimly. "Rumbletop told me that after the first attack, a strange icon appeared on the control screen. He said it looks like a dancing spider."

"It could be a virus!" Neil said, sitting up straight.

"It sounds as though it might be," Kalman said, glancing at Neil fleetingly. "A spider, spreading an invisible web within Firestar."

Casimir looked worried. "Perhaps I should have done something about it," he admitted, wringing his hands together. "I can't understand why I didn't," he frowned. "Rumbletop's been afraid to touch it in case it brought on another attack and as it didn't seem to affect the machine ... he ... well, he decided to leave it alone."

"A mistake," Kalman pointed out icily.

"Will you come into the mountain and help us?" Casimir asked, rising to his feet. Kalman took a step backwards. "You have Alasdair Rothlan in the mountain," he answered. "He's more than capable of tracking down Malfior. You don't need me!"

"Kalman!" Casimir pleaded.

It was to no avail. Prince Kalman had delivered his message and muttering the words of a spell, he hexed himself out of Hughie's kitchen.

30. The spider icon

"So you see," Prince Casimir said grimly, as he finished relating Kalman's story of Malfior and the giants, "we must get rid of this ... this Malfior. If what Cri'achan Mòr said is the truth, then it's hidden inside Firestar."

"But *is* it the truth?" queried Lord Alarid, sitting back in his chair and waving a hand casually. "I mean ... the whole story sounds totally fantastic!"

"Prince Kalman *must* be mistaken," Lord Alban frowned, shaking his head. "We know, indeed, that the giants have risen but how could any evil thing grow within Firestar without its knowledge?"

"Quite impossible!" Lord Dorian declared. "I don't believe a word of it! Firestar would sense it immediately!" At this, there was a murmur of agreement from the other lords. Prince Kalman's tale, they decided, eyeing one another understandingly, was no more than a faery story.

Lord Alarid voiced the general opinion. "How can you think that we'd ever believe such a tale, Casimir?" he said, his voice rising slightly. "We sit here, relaxed and happy, and you come along, deliberately, it seems, trying to spoil our pleasure! It has been a worrying time for all of us — but now that the force that attacked us has been destroyed, we have nothing to worry about. Like you," he declared forcefully, "we feel Firestar's relief within us."

"But surely it would be in Malfior's interest to have us think that?" the MacArthur pointed out, looking to Lord Rothlan for assistance, wondering if their thoughts had been working along the same lines. Amgarad flapped his wings and even Arthur looked interested.

Lord Rothlan eyed Lord Alarid grimly, his brain working swiftly. He believed Kalman's tale implicitly and, like the MacArthur, could see the cunning of Malfior at work. It had obviously succeeded in lulling the lords into a false sense of security. "The MacArthur's right," he said. "Don't you realize, Lord Alarid, that Kalman's story is the truth. He's not telling lies! Not making anything up! What happened to him was real. This ... this Malfior is a threat and Firestar is in danger."

"You are quite mistaken, Alasdair," Lord Alarid began, "we all know that ... that ..." He didn't finish the sentence, however, but halted stumbling in the middle of it, as a strong wave of surprise and anger swept over him.

Firestar had, at last, woken to its danger and was taking a hand in matters. It had no hesitation in making its feelings felt, either, for it instantly washed away their comfortable feeling of false security, leaving them worried, anxious and more than a little afraid. Nevertheless, there was also a reassuring sense of grim determination. Firestar had put itself on a war footing. It was going to fight the enemy.

In no doubt, now, of the gravity of the situation, the Lords of the North looked at one another in fear and amazement. How could this have happened?

"I apologize, Prince Casimir," Lord Alarid said, still looking slightly stunned at the turn of events. "I should never have doubted you. Please forgive me ... I don't know what I was thinking of ..."

"You're not to blame, Lord Alarid," Lord Rothlan interrupted swiftly. "Malfior was influencing your thoughts — all our thoughts, if it comes to that!"

The MacArthur nodded in agreement.

"Looking back on things," Lord Rothlan continued, "I can see now that Malfior's been fooling *us* as well as Firestar." He met Lord Alarid's thoughtful gaze. "Why didn't you listen to Prince Casimir when he told you how important it was to stop the Cri'achan?" he demanded.

"I ... I ... well, it didn't seem important at the time ..." Lord Alarid's voice trailed off.

"Exactly," Lord Rothlan said. "*It didn't seem important.*"

"You're right, Alasdair," Prince Casimir added, sitting up. "It must have been Malfior all along! And looking back on things, I'm sure it frightened the hobgoblins into doing nothing about the spider icon as well. And *I*," his hand slapped the arm of his chair in anger, "*I* let myself be influenced by them!"

"Don't blame yourself, Casimir," Lord Dorian interrupted. "We were all affected."

Prince Casimir suddenly looked less sure of himself. "There is something else I haven't mentioned," he said, looking at Lord Rothlan hesitantly. "Kalman also told me to ask *you*, Alasdair, to rid us of Malfior."

"Me?" Lord Rothlan looked at him in complete surprise.

Casimir smiled wryly. "I know that you have always been rivals in the past ... enemies, even," he added, "but Kalman has never doubted your competence."

The Lords of the North looked at one another with raised eyebrows at this remark. "I think we would all agree with the prince on that," Lord Alarid smiled, "and ... and ..." he paused as a sudden, strong tide of feeling washed over them all in a wave of strength and goodwill. "Firestar ... ," he echoed everyone's thoughts, "Firestar seems to be telling us that he knows of Malfior and is seeking him out." His eyes shone with sudden relief. "Firestar is with us!"

Motivated by the sudden feeling of elation they sat up, their eyes turning to the crystal.

"Perhaps we could have a look at what the giants are doing?" the MacArthur suggested, rising to his feet. "You never know, they might well be re-forming ..."

It was then that Lord Rothlan stood up and bowing low, took his leave of them. *Let the others take care of the giants and the glen,* he thought, making for the stairs that led down to the vast hall where the machine was housed. His smile as he descended was somewhat rueful. *Trust Kalman to land* me *with the job,* he thought ruefully. Nevertheless, he acknowledged that it was a wise choice for none of the other lords would have had a clue how to go about it. It was up to him to access the mysterious icon that Malfior had left behind on the machine.

Rumbletop turned as he approached, looking apprehensive.

"Milord, what news of the giants?" he asked anxiously.

"They're still being held behind the protective shield, Rumbletop," Rothlan replied. "Now, let me have a look at this spider icon of yours. We've got to get rid of it!"

The hobgoblins looked at one another worriedly. "We were afraid to touch it," Rumblegudgeon admitted, looking more than slightly ashamed.

Rothlan didn't bother to explain. "It's a virus," he said shortly, "and it's inside Firestar. We *have* to get rid of it before the giants get to the mountain." And with that, he slid into the chair and, looking at the monitor, clicked on the spider.

The screen promptly turned green and started to roll off reams of numbers and letters that went on and on until they realized that they were being sidetracked.

"Let me try," muttered Rumbletop, "I know something that might work. Come on, Firestar," he muttered desperately as he tapped away at the keyboard. "Do your stuff! The giants are in the glen, for goodness sake!" He scanned the screen anxiously and pressed his lips together in frustration as nothing at all happened. Although the great machine continued to work smoothly with only an occasional hiss of displeasure as he frantically tried to alter its settings, they made no progress whatsoever in accessing Malfior.

"If *only* Firestar would realize that the satellite had left something behind," Rumblegudgeon muttered despairingly, his tendrils growing longer by the minute.

"I think it does, Rumblegudgeon," Lord Rothlan said, scanning the screen. "It's trying to help us. It just doesn't know how."

"Nothing! Nothing at all! Just all these numbers and stuff," Rumbletop looked despairingly at Rumblegudgeon and the other hobgoblins that crowded the hall.

"Lord Rothlan," Prince Casimir called from the staircase, "Lord Alarid would like to speak to you."

Hearing the urgency in his tone, Lord Rothlan looked at Rumblegudgeon. "Keep trying," he instructed, as he got to his feet. "Do anything you can to get rid of the spider."

"What's happened?" Rothlan asked as he climbed the stairs to the Great Hall.

"It's the ghosts from the castle." Casimir said. "They say that Powerprobe has come to life. Chuck's on his computer again!"

Lord Rothlan emerged from the staircase with Prince Casimir in his wake and striding hurriedly through the hall, joined the group that clustered anxiously round the crystal. Lord Alarid glanced at him. "I don't know if it's good news or not, Alasdair," he said, "but Rory tells me that Chuck's on his computer and he thinks he's in touch with the satellite."

"I wonder if Firestar had a hand in that," Rothlan muttered, trying to calm his racing mind as he rapidly calculated the possibilities. "What do you think, Casimir? I have the impression that Firestar's trying to help us despite Malfior putting blocks in the way."

Fired with sudden hope, he returned to the machine but although he worked on it all night, neither he nor the hobgoblins managed to get any nearer to finding Malfior.

Dawn found him exhausted and dispirited — and the news that the giants had re-formed sent his spirits plummeting further. Fear gripped him as he was forced to face the horrifying reality that perhaps he wouldn't be able to destroy Malfior; that perhaps it was too clever for him; that perhaps the giants would succeed ... and claim Morven as their own.

31. The press pack

Aberdeen, a busy city at the best of times, became a hundred times busier overnight as reporters from across the globe descended upon it in droves. The fantastic stone giants that were appearing all over Scotland had become international news and the roads and glens of the Grampian Mountains were soon full of reporters and camera crews anxious to catch a glimpse of the stone monsters. They weren't disappointed, either, for the giants, who seemed to become taller and stronger with each day that passed, were springing up all over the Highlands. Television commentators had a field day as they discussed everything from the reasons for their sudden appearance to their inevitable collapse into landslides. Neither did it take them long to work out that they were all heading eastwards and making for the area around Morven.

"The press people are camping out in the fields near Hughie's cottage," Shona said worriedly as another satellite van rattled past their gates. "Dad's shut the gates so that they don't come and bother us."

Inevitably, of course, a team of broadcasters did turn up at Glenmorven House, for news of the Sinclairs' midnight flight from Glen Garchory was common knowledge in the area and the reporters were adept at sifting through local gossip for a story. Hearing the doorbell ring, Ian Ferguson shrugged. "Maybe if I tell them what I know they

might go away," he said, looking at his wife hopefully.

The cameras were on him as he answered the
door and soon he was telling them about their midnight visitors. "The Sinclairs' farm is in the next
glen," he explained, looking into the camera. "The
weather was stormy. A bit like it is today, actually,"
he said, looking up the glen where black clouds
were gathering.

Kate Cameron who was interviewing him, followed his glance and shivered suddenly. "And what
made them realize that there were giants in the
area?"

"Apparently, there was a sudden, tremendous
noise," Ian said. "It woke them up and when they
looked out of the window, they saw the giants
heaving themselves off the sides of the mountains." He tailed off as an eerie growling noise
roared through Glenmorven. "That's the noise he
described," Ian continued, looking suddenly apprehensive. "The noise the giants make when they're
talking. It looks as though there must be more of
them around."

So strange and fearsome was the sound, that
James, the cameraman, turned quite white and
the world heard Kate's terrified intake of breath
as they all turned to look up the glen.

"We think the giants might be close by," she said
into the microphone in a voice that was half-scared
and half-excited. What a scoop, she thought, to be
around when the giants were actually forming.
"We'll leave this interview for the present and go
further up the glen so that we can have a better

view of what's happening. We think the giants are coming!"

She looked speculatively at the four children who had been standing quietly to one side as the interview had started. *Odd,* she thought. *They don't look the least bit scared. I wonder why?*

"Aren't you scared?" she queried laughingly, holding out the microphone to a pretty, red-haired girl who was clutching a kitten. Great shot, she thought. Just what the viewers want to see. Children and animals always went down well.

Shona shot a cautious glance at Neil and didn't quite know what to say. "I think we're more excited than scared," she said.

Kate's eyes flickered. She hadn't been a reporter for years not to sense that there was a story in the children. The parents seemed genuine enough but she'd bet her bottom dollar that the kids knew a lot more than they were letting on and, as they moved off, she gave Shona a friendly but shrewd look that told her exactly what she was thinking.

The noise grew in volume as they all hurried into the garden. Ian Ferguson, after a quick glance up and down the glen, breathed a sigh of relief. "The noise is being carried on the wind. They're not in Glenmorven yet," he announced, "they're still on the other side of the ridge." And he pointed between the hills to where the ridge loomed dark against the lowering sky. Then they saw them; the towering shapes of giant, stone men, crashing themselves against the protective shield that the Lords of the North had put in place.

One of the broadcasting team ran breathlessly

up to them. "Kate, Kate, come this way," he
gasped. "The press 'copter's coming in. They've
got Harvey Mason on board," his voice sounded
awed as he mentioned the name of the famous TV
presenter. "They're going into the next valley and
want you with them: you ought to get some great
shots."

Everyone crowded across the road and scanned
the sky as a clattering noise in the air announced
the arrival of the helicopter. It landed more or less
in front of the house on the rough ground beside
the burn. Kate was talking into her microphone all
the way as she ran towards it with her cameraman
trailing her.

It was only when the helicopter took to the air
that Clara grabbed Neil's arm.

"Stop them," she cried. "Stop them, Neil!"

"Don't worry, Clara," Shona's mother said,
"I'm sure they'll keep well out of the way of the
giants."

Lewis was the first to realize what she meant
and ran down the slope to the banks of the burn
with the others streaming behind him, shouting
and waving their arms at the helicopter.

They were too late, however, and as it banked
away and headed for Glen Garchory, Kate Cameron
saw them and waved back. Maybe she had been
mistaken, she thought. They were just kids, after
all, excited and a bit overawed by the television
crew. She looked away and they slipped from her
mind as the helicopter soared over the peaks of
the mountains and headed for The Valley of the
Giants.

"We're too late," Clara almost wept.

"Too late for what," Shona asked, panting and out of breath as she followed the others in their mad dash.

"Look at it," Neil said pointing to the whirling rotors of the helicopter. "Just look at it! Don't you *see*, Shona?" He put an arm round her shoulder and squeezed her. "It's too awful to think about," he said, his eyes following the ever decreasing shape of the sky 'copter, "but the giants don't know what helicopters are, do they? They'll think it's a dragon. And ... well, you know what they did to Arthur!"

32. The Valley of the Giants

"Good Lord! Just look at the size of them!" The helicopter circled high over a valley that seemed chock full of giants.

"We're now flying over what I think I might call 'The Valley of the Giants,'" Kate said into the microphone. "Down below I can see dozens of them; huge, giant figures of stone. We're going to fly a little lower so that we can give you a better view of them. Can we do that, Bill?" she asked the pilot.

"No problem," was the answer as they circled lower and lower.

"The giants are making a terrific racket," Kate informed viewers. "You might be able to hear their voices above the noise of the helicopter."

It was a strange sound, for the giants talked in an unearthly, growling roar. They could hear it over the whirr of the rotors. It was an eerie sound that jarred their tense nerves but although they shivered apprehensively, they knew they had to go on.

The story came first, and what a story it was turning out to be! Nevertheless, they were wary and more than a little scared for instinct told them that for the first time in their lives they were in totally uncharted territory. The giants had a tremendous presence and were more than things to be gawped at on a TV screen. It was with a great effort that Kate managed to keep her voice steady and speak calmly.

"The giants have gathered at the end of the valley but although they seem to be pushing forward, they are making no move to enter Glenmorven. Not yet, anyway."

It was then that viewers around the world had a stunning shot of the huge stone figures looking towards a sunlit mountain that lay bathed in glorious light while the sky around was black with cloud.

The roars of the giants increased as they milled around on the ridge, growing more and more frustrated at the invisible shield that blocked their way into Glenmorven. Again they turned and vented their anger on the mountains, tearing rocks and boulders from their slopes.

"Shall we go down closer and get a better look," Kate suggested breathlessly, knowing that her viewers would expect it. "That's better. Now that we're closer to them, I can tell you that they're pretty huge. The size of a block of flats at least, wouldn't you say, Harvey?"

"At least," he agreed, "enormous things! They seem to be made of a mixture of rock, stone and earth but what *is* amazing is that they can walk and move their arms."

"They seem to be throwing stones about," Kate said as they swooped down. "Not at one another, though. Just chucking bits of the mountain around."

"They seem to be able to see," Harvey said, peering downwards, "but I can't see their eyes ..."

The pilot obligingly flew even lower and as he did so the noise of the rotors sounded loud above the voices of the giants. There was a sudden hush as all the giants stopped dead, turned their heads upwards and looked at the helicopter.

"Dragon! Dragon!" they roared in their growling tongue and as the wave of angry sound hit the helicopter, those inside it very quickly decided that it really was time to move out.

"Whoops!" Harvey said. "Bad move! Get us out of here, Bill!"

The pilot didn't need to be told. He went up almost vertically and it was just when they were breathing a sigh of relief at having got out of a sticky situation that the first slab of rock flew past them.

The cameraman, to give him his due, kept his camera rolling and audiences around the world sat up, suddenly horrified, as they saw roaring hordes of furious giants lobbing huge rocks at the helicopter.

"We're in a bit of a difficult situation here," Kate tried to keep her voice calm. "Get us out of here, for goodness sake, Bill! They're chucking rocks at us!"

Fortunately for those inside the helicopter, the giants' aim hadn't improved with practice. They were still rotten shots. Indeed, they had as much success with the helicopter as they'd had with the dragon and, if the truth be told, a cross-eyed, three-legged camel could have done a lot better.

"It just needs one of these rocks to hit the rotors and we're goners," Bill shouted above the roar of the engine.

It wasn't a lucky shot that hit the helicopter,

however. It was a new giant emerging from the mountainside. It rose up, tearing itself from the slopes in a flurry of stones and earth and got to its feet just in time to meet the helicopter as it dashed for safety. They met face to face.

It was so sudden that there wasn't a lot the pilot could do — and he could see from the look of surprise on the giant's face that it was just as taken aback as he was. Bill threw the helicopter frantically to one side and would have made it to safety if the edge of one of the rotors hadn't clipped the giant's shoulder.

That did it. Kate screamed and shut her eyes as the crippled helicopter fell out of the sky. White-faced newscasters in London could only watch in horror as the camera revealed a whirling kaleidoscope of sky, mountain and glen.

The headlines, needless to say, were immediate and predictable:

BREAKING NEWS: PRESS HELICOPTER CRASHES IN VALLEY OF GIANTS

The expected crash, however, didn't come and she opened her eyes as Harvey shook her. "The giant's caught us," he said urgently. And, looking through the perspex bubble of the cabin, they saw that the giant had one hand underneath the skids and the other on the rotor blades above their heads.

Shaking like a leaf, James picked his camera up and, in a trembling voice, Kate started to speak. "We don't quite know what the giant plans to do with us," she said, hanging onto a strap as they slipped haphazardly from side to side as the giant walked across the glen. "Perhaps he thinks we're some sort of new toy ..."

The giants in the valley spoke excitedly in their growling voices and parted to let the new giant through. Still holding the helicopter, it walked to the end of the valley and stopped when it came to the magic shield that prevented it from entering Glenmorven. There was an evil leer on its face as it held the helicopter high, knowing that the Lords of the North would be watching.

Inside Morven, the Lords of the North *were* watching. They looked at one another, their faces appalled. This was a side to the Cri'achan that they'd never witnessed before ... nor would ever have suspected.

"Break the shield," Lord Alarid said, looking grimly at the crystal. "Break it or he'll drop the helicopter."

The giants gave a roar of triumph as the invisible shield disappeared and Kate hung on grimly as the helicopter jerked backwards and forwards as the giant carried it to the side of the mountain and placed it carefully on a jutting bluff of rock that looked down onto the ridge.

"The giant seems to have put the helicopter down," Kate said in relief. "Has ... has he gone, Harvey?"

"Hang on and I'll check," he replied, scrambling out of the machine. With a jaunty wave, he walked to the edge of the rocky outcrop, his legs shaking and his heart beating fast. Knowing that James's camera was focused on his back, he daren't show his nerves but nevertheless, he took a very deep breath before looking downwards into the glen. The giants were still there, milling about on the slopes of the ridge, but although they looked his way, they made no move towards him. In fact, they totally ignored him and it was with a feeling of acute relief that he backed away from the cliff edge and returned to the helicopter. "I think it's quite safe now," he said, popping his head inside the door. "We seem to have lost their interest!" Holding out a hand, he helped them down onto the heather and as the pilot looked ruefully at the bent rotors of the helicopter, James moved forward and focused his camera on the ridge.

"What's happening now, do you think?"

"They seem to be lining up, as though they're waiting for somebody," James said, filming the giants that crowded the glen below.

"Look," Kate grabbed Harvey's arm. "Get that shot, James. There, over to your left. Another giant's rising out of the mountains!"

"Gosh, he's huge, isn't he? Much taller than the others."

"It's some kind of ceremony, Harvey. I'm sure of it."

The new giant was something else. Taller, bigger, more regal and more threatening than all the others put together, he walked with steady steps through the serried ranks of giants that lined the ridge.

"He's their king," Harvey whispered.

"The Old Man of the Mountains," agreed Kate, not knowing where the words came from.

"Cri'achan Mòr!" the giants cried. "Cri'achan Mòr!"

Cri'achan Mòr stopped at the head of the glen and as he came within sight of Morven, he halted and with a mighty roar of triumph, raised his great, stone arms to the heavens. All of the giants did the same and crowded in behind him as he stepped down into Glenmorven.

33. Exodus

"Everyone pull out," yelled a technician, waving his arms to attract attention. "The press 'copter's down but they're all okay. Harvey says to clear the glen. The giants have crossed the ridge and they're in an ugly mood."

Nobody needed to be told. They could see the giants crossing the ridge from where they stood. It was a frightening sight as wave after wave of the huge figures loomed up over the ridge and marched on heavy feet into Glenmorven.

"Cripes! Let's get out of here!" gasped a white-faced reporter. There was a mad rush to get into cars, vans, anything that moved and a hassle of frantic hooting, revving and reversing to get onto the road that led out of the glen.

At the castle, Shane looked frustrated as he climbed into the waiting 4x4. "Chuck staying, then?" Sammy asked. Shane nodded and as the ground started to shake under the weight of the giants' feet, he started the engine and took off at speed.

Shane grunted. "I tried to reason with him but he wasn't having any of it!" he said, starting the engine. "I don't think he was even listening!" he said disgustedly as he backed into the driveway.

And this was, indeed, the truth. Chuck had been so absorbed in the stream of data pouring from his computer that Shane's panic-stricken pleas to leave had barely registered. Indeed, such was his concentration that he'd barely looked up as Shane told him what was going on outside. Leave the castle with Powerprobe up and running again? What on earth was he on about? A total no-brainer if ever he'd heard one.

Now, although Chuck hadn't seen the giants, the others had. And it made a difference!

Shane hadn't wasted time arguing. He knew it was pointless. If Chuck wanted to stay, that was his business — but no way was *he* going to hang around.

He put his foot down hard on the accelerator, so that the gravel spurted beneath his wheels, and took off down the driveway at speed.

Sammy looked back out of the rear window as they left the castle grounds and whitened as he saw the huge figures of the giants, fast approaching from the ridge, terrible in their intensity.

The scene of panic was repeated at Glenmorven House.

"Quick ... into the cars you lot," Ian Ferguson snapped as they tumbled out of the door to see the giants marching towards them with huge strides. Neil and Clara looked at one another. Scared as they were, they didn't want to leave, they wanted to see what would happen when the giants reached Morven.

"I wonder what the magicians will do?" Lewis whispered to Clara as they climbed into the back seat of the car.

"Where's Shona?" Helen Ferguson looked round frantically.

"I'm here, Mum," Shona shouted, running up

with Ugly Mug clutched against her. "I couldn't leave her behind."

Her mother smiled, despite herself. "In you get," she said, "or the giants will be stepping on us!"

"Look," Neil said, excitedly. "There's the 4x4 from the castle. Shane and his lot are pulling out, too."

"I'm not surprised." Ian Ferguson remarked as he turned out of the driveway and settled in behind the Americans.

Lewis craned his neck. Shane was driving but he couldn't see Chuck's spiky hair among the passengers. "Chuck must still be in the castle," he whispered to Neil.

"He must be mad," Neil whispered back. "The giants are on the warpath. You can tell by the way they're stomping along."

"I hope Hughie's okay," Mrs Ferguson said worriedly from the front seat. "I've been looking out for Clarissa but I haven't seen her at all. Do you think we should go back for him?"

"We can't go back," her husband said grimly. "The giants would be on top of us before we reached his cottage. And we've the children to think of!" He looked through his rear-view mirror and scanned the road behind. It was empty. Maybe, he thought, Hughie didn't want to run away. He was a very old man. Perhaps he'd decided just to take his chance.

Racing along at the head of the convoy, the television crews were on their mobiles and despite the dangers the giants posed were determined not to pull out completely. Still anxious to get footage of the giants, they'd slowed down as they came to a passing place at the head of the glen. "This is as far as we go," the producer snapped, jumping down from his jeep. "Offload the gear and get over there," he pointed to a high bluff of rock that gave them a clear view of Morven. "We ought to have a grandstand view from there!"

"Please stop, Mr Ferguson," Neil urged, seeing the cameramen puffing up the steep slope. "The TV people are right. The giants are heading for Morven. They won't come this far. Let's stop and see what happens!"

"Yes, pull in, Ian," his wife urged. "We're far enough away to be safe."

They clambered out of the car and shivered as the wind hit them. The lay-by gave them a spectacular view and they gasped as they saw the giants approach Morven, their roaring voices carried on the wind.

Shona gripped Clara by the arm as they watched them near Hughie's cottage. As it happened, all the houses in the glen were safe, even Jenni's house in Glen Garchory, for the Lords of the North had put a protective shield round them so that no harm would come to them. The children didn't know this, however, and their hearts were in their mouths as they watched the giants approach. Set in a dip in the road, they were afraid that the giants mightn't see the little cottage and tramp all over it. The giants, however, sensed the protective shield round the cottage and avoiding the belt of trees round the little house, lumbered past. Seeing this, the children breathed again as they saw that, for the moment at least, Hughie was safe.

The castle, however, reared high and unmistakeable in a stretch of open ground. The giants saw it and much to their relief, circled it carefully. Glenmorven House, with its sheltering trees was also given a wide berth as the giants converged triumphantly on the mountain.

Shona gave a gasping sob as the others looked at one another aghast. Why weren't the Lords of the North doing something to stop them?

34. Desperate measures

It had been Casimir, in the end, who had persuaded Lord Alarid that they desperately needed Chuck's help; for despite Rothlan's best efforts, the machine was still pouring out the same, meaningless jumble of data. But Alarid, wary of Chuck's motives and terrified of Powerprobe, had dithered and it was only when he had been forced to break the protective shield round the glen to save the people in the helicopter that he'd had to give in — for it was then that they had all ganged up on him.

After all, Prince Casimir had pointed out forcefully, with Cri'achan Mòr leading the march on Morven, it really didn't matter *who* came into the mountain! With no protection against the giants, Chuck was now their only hope!

Lord Rothlan had been quick to act and before Lord Alarid could even think of changing his mind, had promptly hexed himself into the castle.

Now, he gazed at Chuck assessingly, hoping against hope that he could perform miracles. They needed his help badly and time was short!

Chuck stiffened and looked up from his computer as he felt the presence of a figure at his elbow and turned fearfully round. It just had to be one of the ghosts, he thought, looking at the old-fashioned velvet robes and ruffled shirt. Just like the pictures in the portrait gallery upstairs.

"Who ... are you? Are you one of the ghosts?" he whispered through a throat that had gone suddenly dry.

"I'm not a ghost, Chuck," Rothlan said to him. "My name's Alasdair Rothlan and I'm a magician. I've come here to ask for your help."

Chuck looked at him blankly. A magician! He wasn't sure this made his situation any better. Ghosts were one thing and magicians, quite another and although this apparition didn't seem the least bit threatening, he nevertheless swallowed hard and brought his intelligence to bear. It provided poor comfort. Magicians, he reckoned, could be both dangerous and awkward.

"Ask for my help?" he repeated, a frown shading his eyes. "If you're really a magician," he pointed out, "shouldn't you be able to wave a magic wand, or something?"

"What I need you for can't be solved by wands," Rothlan said shortly. "But if it's magic you want ..." He looked round the hall and his eyes fell on the fan-shaped display of swords, claymores and pikes that had so fascinated Neil. Without any more ado, he straightened his arm and threw a hex at it.

Chuck almost leapt the height of himself as the entire display fell; clattering and clanging onto the stone floor in a ferocious jumble of razor-sharp blades. As he knew just how firmly the display had been screwed into the wall, he swung round and looked at the magician in amazement. Before he could even open his mouth to comment, however, there was another great heaving and clanking as the entire armoury rose from the floor, sailed into the air and once more settled, each piece in its place, back on the wall.

"Well?" Lord Rothlan queried quietly. "Do you believe me now?"

Chuck looked at him, his mouth dry. "What ... what exactly do you want me to do?" he asked.

Alasdair Rothlan smiled in relief. He was a handsome man who had always found it easy to make friends and Chuck found himself relaxing slightly. Apart from the fantastic outfit he was wearing, the magician actually looked like quite a nice chap. Dark-haired with direct, brown eyes; his face was serious but not unfriendly.

"That rock that Shane took from the landslide," Rothlan said. "It was part of a giant, wasn't it?"

"How on earth do you know that?" Chuck gasped.

"The ghosts told me."

"The ghosts? You mean you can see them?" Chuck looked round somewhat wildly.

Rothlan pursed his lips in a wry smile. "They're both here, I assure you," he said, nodding to Red Rory and the MacTavish who were watching them interestedly. "Now, tell me about the rock, Chuck."

Chuck shrugged and leant over to pick it from a shelf. "This is it," he said, hefting it in his hand. "It has somehow been de-magnetised. I thought it was a bit strange but it would explain how the giants managed to rise from the mountains."

Rothlan nodded. "That's why we want you to help us." He paused as the giants thumped their way past the castle windows. "The fact is that you and your satellite have caused us a lot of trouble one way or another. It's your fault that the giants woke up, for a start!"

"*We* woke the giants?" Chuck looked out of the window in alarm and blenched at the sight of the huge figures.

Rothlan nodded. "You did ... although I'm sure you didn't intend to."

Chuck, still gobsmacked at the huge figures crashing past the windows, barely heard him. "I didn't realize they were so huge," he stammered. "They ... they just need to step sideways to demolish this place."

"Don't worry, Chuck. We've put a protective shield round the castle so they won't be able to cause any damage. Now, listen. It was something in your satellite that made all this happen. It not only locked on to the power source that keeps those of us in the magical world alive and nearly killed us in the process but it also woke the giants from their sleep so that they were able to rise out of the mountains and walk. You *must* know what caused it!"

"No, I don't," Chuck shook his head. "That's not part of my job. I've no idea what it could be. Just a minute, though! The lasers! I knew it! Professor Jezail was wrong all along." He slapped his hand on the desk of his computer. "I always thought there was a virus ..."

Lord Rothlan froze. "Professor *who*?" he demanded in a somewhat strangled voice.

"Jezail," Chuck answered. "He worked with us on Powerprobe. Brilliant chap!"

Lord Rothlan swallowed. "Indeed," he said in a whisper, hardly able to take in the knowledge that Lord Jezail, of all people, had been involved in such a dastardly scheme.

"Are you all right?" Chuck asked somewhat anxiously, as the magician looked as white as a sheet.

"No, not really," Rothlan admitted. "You've just given me the most dreadful shock."

"About Professor Jezail?"

"Jezail," Rothlan smiled sourly, "is no more a professor than a fly in the air. He's a magician! And a powerful magician at that!"

"He knew his stuff, though," Chuck objected.

"I'm quite sure he did," Lord Rothlan answered, "and I hope you can remember some of it for the virus left an icon like a dancing spider on our screen."

"You have a computer inside the mountain?" Chuck looked amazed.

"Er ... well, yes, I suppose you *could* call it that."

Chuck took a deep breath and looked suddenly excited. Here, he thought, was his chance to get into the mountain at last. "If you like, I'll see what I can do to fix things," he offered.

"Very well," Rothlan said slowly, "but I warn you. When we bring you back to the castle, you'll have no memory of us."

"I don't mind," Chuck said with a grin, "I'm desperate to see what the inside of the mountain's like." He cringed suddenly at the roaring voices of the giants as they tramped round outside and met Rothlan's eyes fearfully. "Come on, let's get a move on! If we're going to get rid of them, it has to be now!"

Rothlan held out both his hands. "Hold my hands," he instructed, "and I'll take you with me into Morven."

And in an instant, they were there, inside the mountain. Chuck barely had time to look in wonder at the awesome sweep of the cavern, the silver thrones, the fearsome dragon that lifted a horned head at his approach and the fabulously dressed Lords of the North who bowed politely as Lord Rothlan swept him swiftly down a long spiral of wide, shallow steps that led into another cavern. It was dominated by a huge, gleaming machine that was nothing like anything Chuck had ever seen before.

And then he saw them and stopped abruptly. The aliens!

The hobgoblins had turned in surprise as Lord Rothlan came hastily down the staircase and almost died of shock when they saw that he was followed by a human. Their goat-like little faces looked totally flabbergasted, their slanting, yellow eyes panicky and their tendrils started sprouting at a furious rate.

"Calm down *at once*," Casimir ordered sternly as Rumbletop and Rumblegudgeon clung anxiously to his robes. Prising their fingers loose, he stepped forward to meet the newcomer with a smile of relief.

"Well, Alasdair?" he said, raising an eyebrow as introductions were performed.

"Chuck's going to try to access his satellite on our machine."

"It's called Powerprobe," Chuck said, trying to take everything in at once. Whatever he had expected, it certainly hadn't been anything like this. It was all quite incredible; the humungous machine, the little goat-like creatures and the fantastically attired occupants of the mountain.

Seeing the consternation on Rumbletop's face, Lord Rothlan took him by the hand and drew him forward. "This is Rumbletop," he said. "He's the hobgoblin in charge of the machine and very shy so you must excuse him if he's a bit nervous of you."

The hobgoblin looked so scared that Chuck squatted down so that their eyes were level. Rumbletop was fascinated and couldn't take his eyes off Chuck's spiked hair. Chuck burst out laughing and Rumbletop jumped back.

It was enough, however. The ice had been broken and Chuck slipped into the chair by the control panel, listening to Rumbletop carefully as the mountain shook from the force of the attacking giants.

"Do something quickly," Prince Casimir said suddenly as the great machine started to vibrate violently and red lights flashed warningly. "Look, the giants are taking energy from Firestar! It will make them even more powerful. You must block it."

"They're bypassing the machine," Rumbletop said, almost in tears.

"Why don't you just shut everything down for a while?" Chuck asked, his mind rapidly turning over a variety of possibilities.

"That would kill us all," Casimir said, his face

white and strained. "Our very lives depend on Firestar."

"Where's this spider icon you were telling me about?" Chuck asked sharply, shocked at the rigid look of control on Rothlan's handsome face.

Rumbletop pointed to it with a shaking hand and Chuck bent forward, mind racing. Something, somewhere clicked in his mind and he gave a sigh of relief. But would it work?

"I reckon this Firestar you told me about must be trying to help," he said. "I bet that's why it re-activated Powerprobe and the lasers. The lasers," he repeated, "they must hold the key ... I wonder ... Ah yes, got it!" he muttered. And as Chuck tapped frantically on the keyboard, the huge machine started to rattle, flash and hiss furiously but whether it was his doing or that of the giants he had no means of telling.

It was, had he but known it, Malfior's doing. Given the strength of his power, Malfior had found it fairly easy to run rings round Firestar and Rumbletop's efforts to catch him were ... well, nothing short of pathetic. Chuck, however, was a different kettle of fish and with sudden, dreadful certainty, Malfior realized that whoever was now at the keyboard, knew what he was doing, knew what he was looking for and worst of all, knew how to track him down.

Despite Chuck's knowledge, however, it proved a long and complicated chase. Chuck tried every-thing but Malfior always managed to keep a few jumps ahead of him, skipping desperately here and there, using his computerized brain to jump from program to program to program. As Chuck erased his hideouts one by one, however, Malfior knew real fear as the realization gradually dawned that he was fighting a losing battle. Frantically, he tried every trick he knew but eventually, with a sinking heart and a sense of complete disbelief, he came to the end of his journey. There was only one place left to hide ...

Knowing the end was near, Chuck tapped away furiously at the keyboard. Rumbletop stood by his side, rigid with excitement, his yellow eyes the only thing that moved as he followed Chuck's manoeuvres on the screen while Rothlan and Casimir, sensing that Chuck was on a winning streak, could barely breathe. They knew exactly how much rested on his shoulders.

Chuck gave an exclamation of triumph as Malfior was suddenly revealed to him. "Gotcha!" he muttered, stabbing finally at the keyboard. "Gotcha!"

Chuck didn't hear Malfior's final, despairing cry as he was erased, zapped, wiped out and finished off for good — but underneath the machine, alone in the depths of the mountain, Firestar suddenly pulsed brightly and knew within itself that the strange entity that was Malfior had been overcome.

Chuck flung himself back in his chair with a sigh of relief as he realized he'd done it! Wow! Thank goodness for that! There had been a few nasty moments when he thought he'd never screw the little blighter down. But he'd done it! The virus had been well and truly nailed! He looked round, expecting cheers and words of praise but nothing happened. It was incredible. No one was there.

It was then that Chuck realized that he was alone in the depths of the mountain. He got to his feet and looked around as though expecting the magicians to pop out from behind the machine. Even the little hobgoblins had vanished.

It was then that the ghastly, inhuman voice of a siren wailed dreadfully through the mountain.

35. Going, going, gone

The TV cameras followed every move the giants made as they pulled huge rocks and boulders from the side of Morven. "News is coming in to us from other parts of Scotland that giants are rising from mountains all over the Grampians and it looks," the newscaster said in a shaking voice, "as if the giants here are in a particularly aggressive mood."

The assault went on and on, the giants' strange voices rumbling eerily across the glen as they pulled and hauled at the mountainside.

Shona put her head to one side. "Listen," she said so commandingly that everyone fell silent. "Listen, can't you hear it? It sounds like a siren."

"It *is* a siren," one of the technicians said, in puzzled wonder. "Where on earth is it coming from, though?"

It came from inside the mountain. Chuck nearly jumped out of his skin as the noise blared through the cavern. The machine seemed to have gone berserk. And it wasn't only the siren; alarm bells were ringing, lights flashing, the lot! Everything seemed at panic stations. *Now* what was wrong, Chuck thought. Had he pressed the wrong key somewhere? The noise the machine was making was something awful. It clanked and clattered alarmingly until he thought it was going to blow up altogether.

On the hillside, the sound of the siren faded

and wasn't repeated although everyone listened hard. Then the cameraman, looking at the giants through a zoom lens, gave a shout. "Look at the giants! They're dying!"

The Cri'achan trembled as they felt Malfior's passing and grunted in dismay as their power left them. With roars of rage, they found themselves growing smaller and smaller as the pull of the earth drew them steadily to the ground. Desperately, they fought against its strength, trying to regain the previous lightness of movement they had enjoyed before, but to no avail. The onlookers watched in amazement as they shrank and shrank and soon grew too small to see.

"Malfior! Malfior! Where are you?" Cri'achan Mòr roared fearfully. But there was no answer to his cry and as he felt himself start to shrink he called, too, on Lord Jezail, knowing that he would be watching him through his crystal.

"You promised!" he shouted furiously, "you promised me Morven, Lord Jezail!" There was no reply, however, and as he became smaller and smaller, he cursed the day that he'd put his faith in magicians.

Cri'achan Mòr held out to the end but there was nothing he could do. Reduced to a tiny figure, his anger was terrible to see and, as the unrelenting force drew him inexorably downwards, he, too, collapsed in a pitiful tumble of rocks and earth, to sleep forever on the slopes of Morven.

There was a deathly hush as the watchers at the head of the glen realized that the reign of the stone giants had passed. Clara pressed her hands over her mouth and stared round-eyed, while Neil and Lewis looked at one another in relief. It was over. Morven was safe.

"Can we go home now?" Shona asked in a small voice.

Her father put his arm round her. "Of course," he said, looking at his wife in relief, "the giants have gone and something tells me that they won't be coming back."

In the Halls of the Giants, Lord Jezail's black eyes held bitter disappointment as he felt all the powerful magic he had secretly stolen from Firestar, drain out of him. Cri'achan Mòr's fury and Malfior's last despairing cries were as nothing to the painful realization that he, himself, had dwindled in stature. Once more just an ordinary magician, there was nothing he could do; not for Malfior nor the giants. His wonderful plan had failed and such was his anger that he slapped the palm of his hand on the rock table, muttered furiously and getting to his feet, strode up and down the boulder-strewn hall, totally beside himself with rage.

Count Vassili moved forward to look in the crystal and paused in awe as he witnessed the collapse of Cri'achan Mòr and as the tiny figure of the great giant finally disintegrated in a pathetic scatter of small stones, his lips tightened and his blue eyes shone as cold as ice as he regarded his master. What had been done, was done. It was definitely time to go.

His face, nevertheless, was quite impassive as he

spoke. "Master," his voice was cold as he passed a hand over the crystal, shutting it down, "it is time for us to leave ..."

Lord Jezail turned towards him, his frowning face still a mask of disappointment. "It *could* have worked, Vassili," he said, angrily. "I was unlucky, that's all."

"Master," Vassily soothed, "there will be other ways to gain the power of the Lords of the North. Don't worry, you will think of them. But now it's time we left this place for the comfort of Stara Zargana. Master, the citadel awaits your return ..."

"You're right, as always, Vassili," the magician remarked, looking round the roughly hewn cavern of the giants, "it's time to go and," he added, his expression lightening at the thought, "there are, as you say, always other ways ..."

Inside the mountain, Chuck looked again at the monitor where lights continued to blink furiously. Still something to sort out, he thought, and sitting down again, tapped away furiously. He didn't really know how he knew but he had a suspicion that Firestar was guiding him. One by one the lights gradually disappeared from the screen and when the last one flickered and died an icy voice spoke in arctic accents.

"That," it said coldly, "was a *very* nasty experience."

Chuck whirled round and saw that the magicians had reappeared. Both looked totally outraged and the hobgoblins were shaking with fright.

"What happened?" he asked, blankly. "Did I make you disappear or something?"

"More like the *or something*," Prince Casimir snapped, controlling his temper with an effort.

"I'm really sorry," Chuck apologized, wondering if he were about to be turned into a toad or whatever it was magicians did when they were in a temper, "but I'm not used to your ... er, computer."

Lord Rothlan saw his point. His rigid expression relaxed slightly and his lips twitched in a smile as he saw the funny side of the situation. It was quite infuriating, of course and what made it even more irritating was that Chuck would never, ever, appreciate the enormity of what he'd done. It wasn't every day that powerful and important magicians were reduced to the size of grasshoppers. Indeed, he wondered if he'd ever live it down.

"You didn't make us disappear," he said, dryly. "At some stage you must have pressed the wrong keys for you made us grow smaller. We tried to attract your attention but you ... er, didn't look down."

"You nearly stood on me," whispered Rumbletop, looking at Chuck reproachfully.

"Gee, I'm really sorry," Chuck said, looking contrite. He knelt down and held the hobgoblin's tiny hands. "I'm not used to magic yet."

Just how unused to magic he was, became immediately apparent. He almost jumped out of his skin as another magician suddenly appeared out of the blue. To say that Lord Dorian was in a temper, is putting things mildly. He was, in actual fact, totally incandescent with rage.

"What on earth's going on down here, Casimir?" he snapped at the prince. "Have you all gone mad? Somebody," he looked round accusingly, "just hexed us and Lord Alarid, let me tell you, is *absolutely* livid!"

"Whoops!" Chuck thought.

"He's not," Dorian said savagely, "used to being half an inch high! And what's more," he glared at them angrily, "neither am I!!"

Lord Rothlan put an arm round Chuck who had taken a few steps backwards and was staring apprehensively at this new magician.

"Meet Chuck, Lord Dorian," he said, "and say thank you." He gestured round the suddenly silent hall and for the first time they realized that the sound of the giants' attack had ceased entirely. "I don't know how he did it but I think he's just sorted out the Cri'achan for us!"

36. Aftermath

"Hughie's all right," Ian Ferguson said, coming back into the kitchen. "He wasn't worried about the giants. Said that the mountain would look after its own."

His wife shook her head at this remark. "Typical Hughie," she said with some asperity. "And there we were, worrying our heads off about him!"

"I thought he was cutting it a bit fine, myself," Ian agreed as he pulled out a chair and sat at the table. "He says he'll bring Clarissa round tomorrow so that you can take the kids back to Aberdeen." He smiled at Lewis. "We'll phone your house this evening, Lewis, just to check arrangements with your mum and dad. Now, is there any tea left in that pot? I could do with a cuppa."

The telephone rang and Mrs Ferguson went to answer it. "That was Jennifer's dad," she said when she came back. "He drove back to check on their house and he says it's fine. No damage to speak of apart from giant footprints all over the hillside. And Jenni says to say goodbye to you two," she smiled at Neil and Clara, "and says she'll see you at school on Monday, Lewis."

"School," Neil groaned. "I'd forgotten all about it!"

"I'm not surprised," Mrs Ferguson laughed. "You've had quite an exciting holiday what with the giants and all."

The children smiled politely and eyed one

another across the room. It was just as well, Shona reckoned, that she didn't know just *how* exciting.

"How about taking a walk before dinner so you can say goodbye to the mountain," Mrs Ferguson suggested.

"Great idea," approved Lewis, "and we can see what's left of the giants as well."

A quarter of an hour later, they left the house and, crossing the burn, headed for the mountain. The scattered remains of the giants littered the slopes in a mess of smallish stones.

"The landslides are nothing like as big as I thought they'd be," Neil remarked, casting an eye over the slopes. "When you think of the number of giants there were, you'd think the whole mountain would be covered in debris!"

"They grew smaller, remember," Shona said. "Maybe that's why."

Suddenly, Clara grasped at her firestone. "My firestone feeeeeeels heavy," she said looking at Neil in startled surprise. The words were hardly out of her mouth when she found herself inside the mountain, standing in front of the Lords of the North with Neil, Lewis and Shona, beside her.

"Bow," whispered Lewis.

Lord Alarid beckoned them forward. "Welcome to Morven," he smiled. "We thought we'd celebrate our victory over the Cri'achan by inviting you to dinner."

Everyone was there. Arthur breathed a long sparkling burst of fire as he saw Neil and Clara and Archie grinned and waved.

It was Chuck, however, who caused the sensation.

Lewis saw him first and grabbed Neil's arm. "Chuck!" he gasped. "Look, he's over there beside Lord Rothlan!"

Clara and Shona looked at the two boys in amazement. "Who's Chuck?" they both asked together as Lord Rothlan, catching Lewis's eye, brought him over.

Neil and Lewis had the grace to look slightly ashamed for on their return from the castle, they'd decided not to tell the girls of their visit. Although Shona's anger at not being allowed onto Morven had drifted from her mind in the excitement of the past few days, it was still, Lewis had felt, simmering beneath the surface. Had Chuck agreed to let her onto the mountain it would have been fine but as he hadn't ... well, neither of them had wanted to stir up old grudges.

"He's one of the Americans from the castle," Neil muttered hastily. "I'll tell you about him later."

"Chuck has been absolutely wonderful," Lady Ellan said, joining them. "He saved us from the giants!"

"*And* managed to zap the virus out of Firestar," her husband added.

Chuck gave Lewis and Neil a very odd look. The last thing he had expected was to see them mingling with magicians inside Morven and he said so.

"It's a long story," Lewis admitted with a grin, "and quite unbelievable, really."

"Try me," Chuck answered. "I'm getting used to the unbelievable!"

Shona, meanwhile, gave a gasp of delight as she saw that Hughie had been invited as well. Indeed, he seemed to have been in the hill for some time as he was deep in conversation with Prince Casimir and the MacArthur. She was just about to rush over to talk to him when Neil grabbed her arm. "Not yet, Shona," he warned. "Look at their faces. I think Hughie's telling them about Prince Kalman. If I were you, I'd wait till he comes over."

It was then that Amgarad landed, in a flap of wings, on Clara's shoulder. Lady Ellan smiled as the huge bird bent its head and pulled gently at Clara's hair. After Lord Rothlan, Clara was definitely his next favourite person.

"We're so pleased to see you all," she said. "We've had quite an exciting day what with one thing and another! Did you see the giants?"

"We were watching from that cliff at the head of the glen," Shona confessed. "It was terrifying. At one stage we really thought that the giants were going to get into the mountain."

"So did we," Lady Ellan confessed and then broke off as Lord Alarid stepped forward and raised his arms. He murmured some magic words and before them appeared a long table covered in a pure, white cloth. Candles glowed, crystal sparkled, silver shone and a myriad of gleaming dishes appeared, laden with delicious food.

The Rumblegrumbles served the meal, resplendent in fine new clothes. Their waistcoats and trousers were of shiny silver cloth and they were so happy that Firestar had been sorted out that Clara wanted to laugh whenever she looked at them for they all wore their ridiculous goblin grins.

After they had eaten, Prince Casimir told them how Chuck had managed to get rid of the virus that it had picked up from Powerprobe. "It was responsible for the rise of the giants and, fortunately for us, he managed to neutralize it."

There was an outburst of clapping at this. Chuck stood up and bowed, as it was a real tribute of gratitude for all that he'd done. Prince Casimir caught Lord Rothlan's eye with a troubled smile. Malfior had gone and the world of magic had been saved but Chuck's news of Lord Jezail had been devastating.

By the time they had finished chatting and speculating, it was getting late but Lord Alarid's magic spell saved them the long walk back as it landed them just outside Glenmorven House.

"Well, did you say goodbye to Morven?" Helen Ferguson asked as they came into the living room.

"Yes, we did," nodded Clara.

"And we saw what was left of the giants," added Shona.

"And what was that?" her father queried, looking up from his newspaper. "Loads of rocks and stones?"

"No, not as much as I thought," she said. "I was expecting massive landslides, but there were just drifts of small stones."

"It was rather sad, really," Shona added. "The giants must have been very small when they died."

"Well, go and wash your hands, now that you're back. Your mother's made you a Chinese stir-fry for dinner."

"How lovely," Shona glanced at the others and, with an effort, managed to look enthusiastic. "My favourite food," Neil said bravely, eyeing Clara and wondering how on earth he was going to manage to eat another meal.

37. The MacArthurs

"I liked your new friends, Clara," Arthur said as she perched herself comfortably in the crook of his arm.

Clara smiled. "Mmmm ... but it's nice to be back in Arthur's Seat with old friends, too," she said, glancing round the Great Hall where George Tatler and Sir James sat talking to the MacArthur.

Neil, sitting beside her, nodded in agreement as he held his arm out so that Cassia, a large black crow, could perch comfortably on it. Her mate, Kitor, however, landed in a flap of wings on Clara's shoulder and nibbled her ear gently with his beak. Hearing of all their adventures up north, he wished that he had gone to Morven with them.

"Who is Shona again?" John MacLean asked, trying to sort out all the new names in his head.

"Shona is in Lewis's class, Dad," Neil explained, "and Jennifer is a year below them. She lives in the next glen to Shona, that's how they're friends."

"That was the glen you rescued us from, Arthur." Clara shivered as she remembered the giants. She looked at Jaikie and Hamish. "It's a pity you weren't there," she said, "for it was the most fantastic thing you ever saw. The giants were chucking huge rocks about like confetti and when they started to grow tall, I thought they were going to reach out and catch Arthur! I didn't realize he'd put a spell on them."

Arthur blew smoke down his long nose as if to

say that it would take much more than a giant to catch him. Kitor coughed and flapped his wings. He always kept a wary eye on Arthur who had an alarming tendency to blow fire and smoke at the drop of a hat.

Archie grinned. "I must say, it's great to have you both back in Edinburgh. It's been a bit boring here after our adventure with the giants."

"Is there any news from Lord Rothlan?" Neil asked, looking at the MacArthur hopefully.

"Lord Rothlan and Lady Ellan have already left Morven," the MacArthur answered. "They're back at Jarishan now."

"Amgarad will be pleased, then," Clara smiled. "He didn't like being cooped up in the mountain."

"What was it like, Archie, flying with Amgarad?" Neil asked, remembering that Archie had merged with the eagle to fly back to Morven.

"It was the most amazing thing," Archie said, his eyes bright with pleasure at the memory. "The strength of his wings was amazing. It was too short a journey, though, for Morven was only a few miles away. It was really a dream come true. I've always wanted to fly with the eagles, you know."

Hamish met Clara's eyes and smiled. "We know," he said pointedly.

"Thank goodness you managed it, Archie," Jaikie said. "Maybe you'll stop pestering us now!"

"I wouldn't count on it," Hamish observed. "Just wait until the next eagle comes along, eh, Archie!"

Sir James looked at the MacArthur, sitting on

his carved, wooden chair and interrupted the exchange with a smile for Archie had already told him several times of his wonderful flight. "Archie's been telling us about the giants, too, Neil. It sounds as though you and Clara had a very exciting time."

"If it hadn't been for the Americans and their wretched satellite," Tatler snorted, "the virus would never have got into Firestar in the first place and none of it would ever have happened."

"It caused a lot of hardship," Sir James admitted. "Most of the glens up north have been cleared but it'll be a while before the Highlands really get back to normal." He stretched his long legs and relaxed comfortably on a long divan.

"I see from the newspapers that everything's been put down to extreme weather conditions," John MacLean said.

"Yes," Neil added. "No mention of the giants these days, which is a bit surprising given the headlines they caused!"

Sir James looked at the MacArthur searchingly and smiled slightly. "Did the Lords of the North have anything to do with that, by any chance?" he queried.

The MacArthur nodded. "I should imagine so," he said. "Such things are best forgotten, don't you think?"

Sir James nodded in agreement. "Global warming's probably as good an excuse as any," he said approvingly. "But what about the Americans? What are they doing now?" he queried. "Does anyone know?"

"Prince Casimir tells me that they're on their way back to the States," the MacArthur replied. "Powerprobe's been behaving very erratically and he reckons it won't be long before they shut the whole project down."

"That's wonderful news," Tatler sat up and then looked at him shrewdly. "Did the Lords of the North have a hand in that as well?"

"Well ... yes," the MacArthur admitted, smiling slightly, "but there were other factors as well. Apparently, Lord Robertson saw what was happening on television while he was in Canada and was so upset that he cut his holiday short. The ghosts are delighted to have him back, needless to say!"

"They didn't like the Americans much," Neil said with a grin.

"Ah, but that was because they wanted to get inside the mountain," the MacArthur said. "Rory and the MacTavish didn't approve of that at all! It's understandable! Now, if they'd been normal tourists, I think the ghosts would have kept themselves to themselves and bothered no one."

"Shona will be over the moon to see Lord Robertson again," Clara smiled, "*and* she'll be able to climb Morven to her heart's content over the summer holidays!"

Arthur blew a cloud of smoke down his long nose that sent Kitor and Cassia coughing. "Give over, Arthur," Archie complained, waving his hands around. "The MacArthur's pipe is bad enough without you joining in!"

"Come on, you two," John MacLean said, looking at his watch and getting to his feet. "It's getting late and you still have homework to finish, haven't you?"

Neil nodded guiltily.

Listening to the tale of their adventures, his father had already decided to give his wife a very watered down version of the whole affair. No need to worry her unduly and the children, after all, were safe and sound. His mind veered towards other things as they called their magic carpets, for his brother, David was still seriously ill and he planned to drive down to the Borders the following morning.

Clara looked at Neil and sighed; after dealing with dragons, giants and magicians it was a bit much, she felt, to be landed with homework.

Sir James and Tatler rose to leave as well and as the magic carpets sailed across the Great Hall the MacArthur eased himself back gently in his chair and reached for his pipe. It had been a fairly desperate time but they seemed to have got through it without too much trouble. Firestar was back to normal, the Cri'achan had returned to the mountains and the Lords of the North were safe.

Nevertheless, he shifted uneasily in his chair. It was the knowledge that Lord Jezail had been mixed up in it all, that worried him. The Sultan, too, had been startled at the news and had already arranged a meeting in Turkey. Maybe Prince Casimir, who had visited Ashgar more than once, would be able to throw some light on the matter. But he doubted it. Jezail had always been a law unto himself. And, as Arthur curled lazily by his side, the MacArthur thoughtfully lit his pipe. More trouble brewing, he mused with a sigh ...

38. Jelly Bean giants

"Oh look, Hughie," Shona said, sitting up in her chair. "There's a hobgoblin at the door."

"It's Rumbletumble," Hughie grinned as the little hobgoblin's head appeared shyly round the kitchen door. "Come in, then," he said. "Come in. The cakes aren't quite ready yet so you'll have to wait for a few minutes."

Rumbletumble was followed by Rumbletop and Rumblegudgeon all of whom had sniffed the tantalizing smell of newly-baked cakes from the hillside. Their tiny hooves made a clicking noise on the tiles as they headed for the cushions in front of the fire.

"Shona," Rumbletop said in surprise as they crowded round her chair.

"It's nice to be able to see you!" Rumbletumble said, smiling.

"It's nice to be able to see you, too," she replied, shaking each tiny hand. "How are you getting on in the mountain?" she asked. "Is Firestar behaving itself?"

There were enthusiastic nods.

"And what about the lords?"

"It's a bit dull now," Rumblegudgeon confided. "Lord Rothlan and Lady Ellan have gone back to Jarishan and Prince Casimir looks sad all the time. He misses his son."

"He's going to Turkey next week," Rumbletop confided.

"Turkey?" Shona looked surprised.

"To visit the Sultan," Rumblegudgeon added.

"Oh, yes. Lewis told me about the Sultan. I'd love to meet him. He sounds fabulous."

"He's very fabulous," Rumbletumble said, keeping a careful eye on the oven. His goat-like little face looked so anxious that Shona bit back a smile.

"The cakes smell lovely, don't they," she said seriously as Hughie put on oven gloves.

"Your favourites, Rumbletop," he said with a knowing smile, taking two baking trays out of the oven. "Coconut surprises!"

Again there was a clatter of hooves as they crowded round, standing on tip-toe, their eyes appearing just above the level of the table.

Rumblegudgeon grasped Shona's hand and pulled her to her feet so that she didn't miss out on the treats. His endearing, ridiculous, goblin grin creased her up but she managed to keep a straight face so as not to hurt his feelings. Hughie dealt out the cakes on little plates, three on each and it was as she thanked him that her attention was caught by a sudden movement on the slopes of Morven.

"The stag!" she said, gazing out the window. "Dad said he'd seen a stag on the hill the other night but I didn't know if it was Kalman's or not."

"I reckon Glenmorven is his home now," Hughie said, turning to look out of the long, low windows that gave onto the slopes of Morven. "He likes the glen and feels safe here. The Lords of the North will always protect him and if the winter gets too bad, well, he can always shelter in the old stable."

The hobgoblins, as usual, ate their cakes in little, delicate bites so that it took them a long, long time to get through each one.

"Have some more, Shona?" Hughie offered.

Shona shook her head. "They were delicious but I'd better not," she said. "Mum's cooking a stir-fry and she says will seven o'clock suit you? Dad's working late most nights but he thinks he'll be home in time."

"Jamie Robertson will be coming too, then," Hughie said as she hugged the hobgoblins and made her way to the door.

Shona's eyes sparkled. "Yes, of course. There's just so much to talk about."

"Aye, he's pleased to be back. He told me that his son and daughter-in-law are coming over in a few months' time."

"We'll have to persuade them to stay," Shona said decisively. "Oh look! There's the stag again." She pointed to the skyline where the great stag with its magnificent head of antlers, stood outlined against the setting sun.

Shona heaved a sigh of great content. "Isn't it wonderful, Hughie," she said. "Glenmorven is back to normal again."

Hughie nodded but once she had gone and the hobgoblins had departed, his eyes strayed once again to the window and the stag outlined against the setting sun. Kalman, he thought with a sigh. An unhappy prince if ever there was one. Where, he wondered, was he now and what was he doing? His eyes dropped sadly as he drew the curtains and turned to add some more logs to the fire.

Then he started in surprise. Prince Kalman sat in one of the armchairs beside the fire, looking at him with an unusual air of diffidence. "I hope I'm welcome, Hughie?" he said, rising to his feet, a touch of arrogance showing in the tilt of his head.

Hmmm, thought Hughie, with a wry smile. He was still as proud as the devil, ready to cast a hex and take off at the slightest hint of rejection. Nevertheless, his kind old eyes softened. "You're always welcome, Prince Kalman," he said, "and well you know it!"

Kalman relaxed and sat down again, reaching for some old newspapers that were full of stories about the giants. "So Rothlan managed to get rid of Malfior," he remarked, turning the pages.

Hughie, who had had the whole story from the hobgoblins, retold what he could remember of their excited chatter. "I think it was the American that did it in the end," he said. "According to Rumbletop, he was a real whiz with computers and even on the machine, seemed to know exactly what he was doing. He was the one that managed to pin Malfior down."

Kalman frowned. "So," he muttered, "it has been destroyed."

"I thought you'd be pleased at the news," Hughie ventured, looking at him oddly; puzzled at his expression. He noted, too, that Kalman seemed to have aged since he last saw him and wondered what was worrying him.

Kalman shrugged. "Of course I'm pleased," he said. "Malfior would have destroyed us all without the slightest hesitation." He paused and looking unusually grim, tapped his fingers on the arm of the chair. "I felt its power, Hughie, when I was in Hell's Glen and believe me, it was possessed of a vicious intelligence."

He laid the newspaper down on a side table, looking troubled, for although Malfior had been destroyed, he nevertheless felt the bitter residue of Cri'achan Mòr's hex. It was like a sickness within him but somehow he couldn't bring himself to tell Hughie. Hughie would pass the news on to his father for sure and he shied at the thought of him knowing.

Seeing his frown, Hughie changed the subject in an effort to lighten the atmosphere. "There's a bit in today's paper that might interest you," he said with a smile, "about the pop stars that brought you over from Argyle. The Jelly Beans! Remember them?"

"Making a hit, are they?" Kalman almost smiled.

"More than that," Hughie grinned, "they made a big splash with their stories of the giants and ... well, since then, they just seemed to have taken off. The publicity they've been given is phenomenal. You wouldn't believe it! Their pictures are everywhere these days. In fact, I think it's tonight that they'll be playing at some massive pop festival."

"Where?" queried the prince.

"Somewhere in England," Hughie answered, turning the pages to find the article, "at a place called Glastonbury. They've made it to the big time," he added, "for they're appearing alongside some really big stars."

Kalman sat up straight. "They can't do that," he said, frowning.

"What do you mean?" Hughie looked startled.

"Just that they'll make *total* fools of themselves!"

"Aren't ... aren't they any good, then?"

"As an act, they're terrible!" Kalman looked upset. "Kenny can't play more than a few chords and Larry's voice is painful, to say the least." He shook his head in frustration. "I can't let them do this, Hughie. I've got to stop them somehow!"

Hughie looked at him in a mixture of approval and some surprise. The prince didn't usually concern himself in the affairs of humans and he wondered what had happened in his travels with the Jelly Beans to put him in such a flap.

Muttering the words of a hex, Kalman turned to the wall of the cottage where a huge picture suddenly appeared. Hughie looked at it in astonishment and lifted his hands to cover his ears as the music of the Glastonbury Rock Festival roared through the cottage. Judging from the noise of the screaming fans, the current stage act was receiving a fantastic reception.

"Where are they?" muttered Kalman as he scanned the stage and the area around it. "Where – on – earth – are – they?"

"There," pointed Hughie. "Over to the right! Look, you can see their hats!"

Sure enough, standing at the side of the stage, ready to go on, were Kenny and Larry. Kalman focused on them and then enlarged them until they filled the cottage wall.

"I think it's just dawned on them that they should never have accepted the invitation," he said exasperatedly as a chalk-faced Larry, his eyes as round as saucers, took in the full of glory of a real rock festival.

"I cannae go on, Kenny," he whispered, his voice shaking. "We're no' good enough. They'll ... they'll laugh us off the stage!"

Kenny looked grim. "I know," he muttered, "but we can't *not* go on. They'll make us! They've paid us a fortune to appear and you know as well as I do that everybody out there is waiting to see us. We're the stars of the show, for goodness sake!!"

"What'll we do? We're on next!" whimpered Larry, grabbing at his sleeve as he saw one of the stage managers moving towards them. "Look, look, Kenny! Look at my hand!" He held out a trembling hand that was shaking violently. "I can't play, the state I'm in." Bleak despair shone in his eyes. "Kenny, what are we going to *do*?"

"*I'll* tell you what you're going to do," Prince Kalman interrupted forcefully.

Kenny and Larry eyed one another in amazement as they heard the sound of the familiar voice in their heads. Their faces lit up like beacons as they stared around, half expecting to see the stag at their elbow.

"You made it, then," Kenny said, "you made it to Morven!"

"You're on next," the stage manager broke in. Kenny and Larry paid him not a blind bit of notice.

"Are you okay?" Larry demanded.

"I'm fine," answered Kalman and the stage manager together.

"Not you," Larry looked at the stage manager in some disgust.

"Look, will you just get on to the stage," the stage manager hustled them forward, hoping that they weren't going to prove awkward. He'd heard them rehearsing and wasn't surprised that they had cold feet but that wasn't his problem. All he had to do was get them in front of the mikes.

The band onstage were bowing and waving to the fans, the noise was deafening and everyone standing in the wings was on a tremendous high. "And now," the announcer said, "now we have what you might call the giant attraction of the evening, fans. The lads that faced death and lived through it! The fabulous, fantastic JELLY BEANS!"

Everyone standing in the wings was now aware of the problem. Kenny and Larry, suddenly jerked back to reality, were, once more, white-faced, rigid and more or less frozen to the ground. The band members coming off-stage took one look at them and went into action. "Hey, there," their lead singer said, "don't worry, just go on and you'll be fine! I'll tell you a secret — we all suffer from stage fright, don't we, lads!" There was a murmur of agreement as they clustered round, nodding encouragingly.

"Do as the man says," Kalman ordered. "Go on and you'll be fine, I promise you!"

"Are you sure?" Kenny whispered through stiff lips.

"Positive," the others said, slapping him on the back.

"You'll perform as you've never done before," Kalman assured them, watching as the announcer beckoned them forward. "Give them a great welcome, fans," he roared, "the fantastic, crazy, wonderful — JELLY BEANS!!"

The wave of cheering died down as Kenny and Larry stood in front of the microphones, clutching their guitars nervously. Kalman, however, didn't let the silence last. He muttered the words of a powerful hex and as it hit them, Kenny and Larry jerked in sudden amazement and automatically went into their routine.

And what a routine it proved to be! There was nothing remotely pathetic about it! It was heady, powerful stuff and as their voices rang out strongly, the audience screamed in response! Kenny looked at Larry and they grinned in rising elation as they belted out another song. The magician hadn't let them down; he'd stood by them and paid his debt.

From then on, the audience went wild; screaming, shouting and yelling as Kenny and Larry dominated the stage. They were a sensation! When the near hysterical fans finally allowed them to leave, they looked at one another in a stupified daze of happiness for hit, had followed hit, had followed hit.

"Well, well," Neil turned down the volume on the TV set as the Jelly Beans left the stage to gales of applause, "who do you reckon was responsible for that, then?"

"Prince Kalman, definitely," Clara answered. "It couldn't have been anyone else."

Neil nodded. "He's made them into stars," he said a trifle enviously. "That was really some performance, you know! They were fabulous!"

Just then, his mobile bleeped imperatively. "It's a text from Lewis," he said, scanning the screen. "He thinks Kalman's behind the Jelly Bean's rise to fame — just like us, and," Neil scrolled down further, "he says that what's really surprising is that Kalman bothered to help them at all."

"He's right there. Kalman's not a do-gooder at the best of times, is he?"

"Mind you," Neil rejoined, his eyes on his mobile as he texted a reply, "anyone would feel grateful to them after what happened with the giants."

"Kalman's not exactly anyone," Clara said, smiling ruefully, "but — well, give him his due, Neil. He's done well this evening, hasn't he?"

She looked thoughtfully at the Jelly Beans as, waving and smiling, they left the stage on a roaring wave of applause. Like everyone else watching, she knew they'd made history that evening and were destined for fame and fortune, stardom and glory.

From its rocky perch on the steep sides of Morven, the stag, outlined dramatically against the full moon, surveyed the gentle slopes of the glen, its eyes searching the hillside for a glimpse of the prince; although it sensed, instinctively, that he had already left — probably for some strange, magic land, far away.

Nevertheless, its heart swelled with pride and affection at the thought of the prince's farewell;

for there, on the rough, heather-clad slopes, he had talked of all they had been through together, the dangers they had faced and the hardships they had endured and had thanked him gratefully.

The stag's brown eyes again swept the glen, resting momentarily on the moonlit turrets of the castle and the gleaming white walls of Glenmorven House, and softening as they saw the half-hidden outline of Hughie's cottage, tucked in its little hollow. It knew that when the cold breath of winter covered the land that there, in the old stable, it would find food, warmth and shelter.

It tossed its head at the thought of everything that had happened, for memories of the giants hadn't quite faded from its mind. But in the end, everything had turned out well; the giants had gone forever, Glenmorven was now its home and one day ... one day, it knew, Prince Kalman would return.

Author's Note

I would like to apologize most sincerely to the children of Ballatar, and the surrounding area, for altering the shape of their mountain to fit in with my tale of giants and dragons, hobgoblins and magicians, and hope that, despite this, they have enjoyed my story.

Anne Forbes, *Dragonfire*

'Brilliant … a book that would be perfect for giving.'
— *Janette Perkins, School Librarian Journal*

Clara and Neil have always known the MacArthurs, the little people who live under Arthur's Seat, in Holyrood Park, but they are not quite prepared for what else is living under the hill. Feuding faery lords, missing whisky, magic carpets, firestones and ancient spells … where will it end? And how did it all start?

Set against the backdrop of the Edinburgh Fringe and Military Tattoo this is a fast-paced comic adventure, full of magic, mayhem and mystery … and a dragon.

Contemporary Kelpies

Anne Forbes, *The Wings of Ruksh*

'For children who have read and enjoyed the Harry Potter series this is a fantastic title with which to continue their journey into the fantasy genre.'
— *Hilary Tomney, School Librarian Journal*

What lurks behind the magic mirrors? How are they connected to the missing Sultan's Crown and what secrets does the mysterious black tower hold?

From an Edinburgh literally cloaked in tartan, through the forbidding Highland hills, Neil and Clara set out on a perilous journey of winged horses and snow witches — and a reluctant broomstick.

Contemporary Kelpies

Anne Forbes, *The Underground City*

'Oozes magic, mystery and adventure'.
— *Sandra Dick, Edinburgh Evening News*

On the eve of his return to Scotland, Lewis Grant is dared to spend the night at the haunted desert oasis of Al Antara. But things don't go according to plan and on Lewis' subsequent arrival in Edinburgh, strange things start to happen.

Set against the spooky backdrop of Mary King's Close, Neil and Clara MacLean find themselves embroiled with the enigmatic Lewis, frightened ghosts, reckless bank robbers and a very cranky djinn.

Contemporary Kelpies